Wrecker

FALLEN LORDS MC
BOOK 4

WINTER TRAVERS

D1526375

Natalie,

Much love!
Thanks for being
so awesome!

4

For questions or comments about this book, please contact the author at wintertravers84@gmail.com

Also by Winter Travers

Devil's Knights Series:
Loving Lo
Finding Cyn
Gravel's Road
Battling Troy
Gambler's Longshot
Keeping Meg
Fighting Demon
Unraveling Fayth

Skid Row Kings Series:
DownShift
PowerShift
BangShift

Fallen Lords MC Series
Nickel
Pipe
Maniac
Wrecker

Powerhouse MA Series
Dropkick My Heart
Love on the Mat
Black Belt in Love
Black Belt Knockout

Nitro Crew Series
Burndown
Holeshot (Coming September 2018)

Table of Contents

1st Chapter of Burndown

Acknowledgements

There have been so many people who joined me on this journey and for one reason or another aren't with me anymore. This book is for everyone who has stuck with me no matter what.

My boys, family, Nikki Horn, my Dirty Bitches, Mayra Statham, Kelly Tucker, my BETAs, and the many people I'm forgetting. Thank you for being part of this amazing journey.

Dedication

LET YOUR CRAZY OUT.

PROLOGUE

ALICE

"Are you having a gathering at the house?"

I clutched the urn that contained the ashes of my mother to my chest. "Um, no." There wasn't anyone to gather at the house. The minister had to see that. Did he think even though no one showed up to the service that they were going to magically appear at my house? No such luck.

The only people who would be gathering at my house were going to be me and the ashes of my mother. A bottle of Jack Daniels was more than likely going to make a special appearance.

"Did you want to come over for dinner, dear? Marilynn and I would love to have you."

I shook my head and swiped at my eyes. "No, I don't want to impose. I'll be fine, Pastor Rye."

He nodded. "If that is what you want, but just remember, the church is always here if you need us."

He patted me on the shoulder and left me standing by the stairs of the church.

The wind whipped around me, tossing my hair and ruffling the hem of my skirt.

I hated this skirt.

My mother had loved it.

I wore it because I knew it would make her smile to see me so uncomfortable.

My mother was my best friend. She could make me smile, and in the next breath, yell at me for eating the last of the pickles.

Yes, pickles. The spicy ones were her favorite. I learned early on to never eat the last one in the jar. Even right before she passed away, she bugged me about the pickles.

Though it was hard for her to remember she didn't have pickles in her room. She didn't have anything in her room besides her bed, a three-drawer dresser, and a small TV.

My mother lived her last days at St. Patrick's Nursing and Rehabilitation.

She had dementia, and on her good days, she remembered I was her daughter. On her bad days, she thought I was just another nurse checking in on her. I stayed with her the most on her bad days, hoping something would click and she would remember who I was.

The day my mother died had been a good day. We laughed about the jar of pickles I had smuggled into her room, giggled when I tripped over the cord to her TV, and smiled when we talked about moving her home with me.

I lied to my mother that day. Promised that she would come home with me. I knew from the past that her good days lasted only so long before she forgot everything and went back to thinking I was a nurse.

The doctors couldn't tell me why my mother lost her memory. No one understood dementia and why it affected some people and not others. There were theories, but that was all they were—theories. Theories didn't help my mother. They didn't give her back her memory of me growing up.

Theories did nothing but make me lie awake at night wondering if I had done something in the past that had somehow fucked with the universe and punished me by taking away my mother.

But no matter how long I laid awake, I never found an answer.

My mom had dementia, and there hadn't been a damn thing I could have done about it.

Now, she was gone, and I was all alone.

All the pickles could be mine, and that was the thing that broke me. I was never going to hear my mom yell at me for eating all the pickles again.

Funny thing was, I would give up all the pickles in the world just to have one more second with her. I missed my momma, and I was never going to be okay with her gone.

*

CHAPTER 1

WRECKER

"I don't know what to do," she sobbed over and over.

I lifted her into my arms, stepped into her house, and closed the door behind me. I didn't know what the hell was wrong or what to do either, but I was going to figure out how to make her stop crying. That was the one thing I couldn't handle coming from her. The light which normally shone from her green eyes was dimmed by the tears falling.

The TV blared some commercial, and all the lights were on in the kitchen and living room. I didn't know what to do with her.

Sit down?

Take her to bed?

Leave?

I was surprised leaving was the third thing that had come to mind. I wasn't one to hang around when there was chick shit going on or there was crying involved. Since I was the only one there, I didn't have much choice but to stay and try to figure out what was going on with Alice.

She hiccuped and wiped her nose on my shirt. "I snotted all over you."

"All good, babe."

She laid her head on my shoulder and sighed. Her breathing evened out, but I could still feel her tears soaking my shirt.

"You wanna talk about it?"

She shook her head.

"What do you wanna do?"

"Nothing," she whispered. "Why are you here?"

"Girls were worried about you. Asked me to stop by on my way back to the club to check on you."

She leaned her head back and looked up at me. "Why were they worried?"

"Hadn't heard from you in a bit."

She scrambled off my lap and stood up. "Uh, I had some stuff going on."

"Why'd you get up?" I didn't think I had said anything to upset her. She asked why I was here, and I told her.

She brushed her hands down her shorts. "Uh, needed to stretch my legs."

I quirked an eyebrow at her. "Come again?"

"I wanted to get up."

I held up my hands. "No problem, babe."

She bit her lip and glanced at the front door. "Uh, so, I'm good."

"This is you being good?" Her eyes connected with mine. There wasn't any light in them. Alice wasn't in there.

"Yes, this is me being good."

I shook my head and crossed my ankle over my knee. "I've seen you a couple of times at the club, babe. This is not you looking fine."

She looked down her body. "Is there a problem with what I'm wearing?"

"Not what I'm talking about." She was wearing a loose shirt with the words "save the chubby unicorns" across her chest and a rhino under it. "Though I have to ask what the hell your shirt even means."

She scoffed. "If I have to explain it, then it's not funny anymore."

"It wasn't even funny to begin with, babe."

"Now I see why you came here. You've insulted my favorite shirt and made me stop crying." She pointed at the door. "You can go now. I have plans."

"What plans?"

She propped her hands on her hips. "Ones that have nothing to do with you."

"Why don't you add me into those plans?" I wasn't ready to leave. Not yet.

She huffed, walked into the kitchen, and started slamming cabinets. "I'm making a drink, and when I walk back into the living room, you need to be gone, Wrecker."

"I thought you would be much more hospitable than this, Alice." I didn't move from the couch. Alice could tell me she wanted me to leave, but I wasn't going anywhere 'til I found out why she was crying before.

"Guess I'm just not in the mood for company."

"And just why is that?" I called. I heard ice cubes hit the bottom of a glass. "Are you making me a drink, babe?"

"No. I'm making *myself* a drink, like I said. If I tell you why I'm not in the mood for company, then will you leave?"

That was a tough one. I wanted her to tell me what was wrong, but what it was had to be something pretty bad. I had to play this just right. "Tell me."

"Promise as soon as I tell you, you'll leave."

Shit. She wasn't going to be easy to work around. "I'll leave."

"Say you'll leave as soon as I tell you."

God damn. "Fine, Alice. As soon as you tell me why you're not in the mood for company, I will leave." I listened to her move around the kitchen, and then she walked back into the living room.

She had a glass filled with amber colored liquor in her hand. She took a sip and nodded to the TV. "See that vasey thing there?"

I did. It was light blue with a light-yellow swirl running through it. "Pretty, babe."

She took a long drink and wiped her mouth with the back of her hand. "That's my mama. She died three days ago." Her voice was flat, as if she just told me the weather. "The service at the church was today. I was the only one there." She drained the rest of her glass and dropped it to the floor. "You can go now, Wrecker."

ALICE

He left.

No word.

Just left.

"Good riddance," I muttered to the empty house. At least, that was what I was going to tell myself. I grabbed my glass off the floor and moved back to the bottle I left on the counter. I heard his bike start up and roar down the street. "Good freakin' riddance," I mumbled again.

I didn't understand why he had even stopped by in the first place.

Why not have Nickel or Pipe come up here? He was worried about me?

Bullshit.

"Karmen and Nikki were worried about me, not Beardilocks." A laugh bubbled out of my mouth. "Good one, Alice."

I refilled my glass and grabbed the huge container of animal crackers that was sitting on the counter. "Whiskey and delicious animal shaped cookies. Not much more a girl could ask for."

I talked to myself. A lot.

All. The. Time.

I was also funny as fuck.

The talking to myself out loud and being crazy funny went hand-in-hand. "Totally funny as fuck." I plopped down on the sofa in the spot Wrecker had vacated and twisted off the blue lid to the animal crackers. I dug around for a cute little elephant and bit off its trunk. "Sorry, little dude." I popped the rest of him in my mouth and reached for the remote to change the channel.

Before Wrecker had arrived, I was in the middle of a mental breakdown while trying to find something to watch. A pickle commercial had come on, and I seriously lost it. After I came home from the service, I had baked a frozen pizza, eaten half of it, fed the other half to the stray dog that hung out under my back porch, then tried to find something to watch on TV. In my quest to find something to entertain me, I had stumbled upon the fact that a pickle commercial was now a trigger for me.

"Loser," I whispered. I sipped on my drink while flipping the channels 'til I settled on some cold case show.

My night was going to be watching mindless TV where the only thing I had to think about was who done it and whether I should move the bottle of booze into the living room.

I hopped off the couch, popped two more ice cubes into my glass, and grabbed the half-full bottle of whiskey. My ass wasn't going to get off the couch anymore.

Whiskey and animal crackers were totally going to be my dinner.

Three hours later, after watching three cold cases get solved by DNA that had been collected at the scene but couldn't be used 'til they fast-forwarded twenty or thirty years because we developed fancy-dancy machines to solve shit like that, I shook my head. Where the hell was I going with this thought?

I unfolded my legs from under me and stretched them out.

I lifted the bottle of whiskey to my lips and grimaced. "Way better cold." I leaned forward to set the bottle on the coffee table, and my world tilted on its axis. I slammed my eyes shut and tried to calm the rolling of my stomach.

Well, I was blitzed.

Mission. Accomplished.

All depressing and crippling thoughts I had about today were replaced with a feeling of floating and the craving for a cigarette. I only smoked when I drank, and didn't you know, I was a drinkin'.

I shakily stood up and tried to remember where I hid my cigarettes. About five years ago, I had been a heavy smoker but had given it up in exchange for ding dongs and any candy bar I could get my hands on when the craving for one would hit.

"Tree stump," I muttered. At least, that's where I thought I hid them. "Only one way to find out." I stumbled over to the door and leaned heavily against it.

Next time I hid them, I was going to at least make it a place inside. Trekking to a tree stump in the backyard when I was a half way into a bottle of whiskey was not ideal.

I threw open the door and swayed as the fresh air hit me. "That's up me sobered." I titled my head. "That's not right," I slurred. I really needed to stop talking out loud to myself. "Makes ya look crazy, Alice."

"Babe."

I jumped, the living shit scared out of me, and fell flat on my face on the porch. I could barely stay on my feet when I was sober, so when I had a few in me, I met the ground quite often. Also, someone calling me "babe" when I had no idea there was anyone there surprised me. "Wrecker?" I looked up and saw him sitting in the rocking chair I had tucked away in the corner of the deck.

"Yeah."

I pushed off the floor and sat up. "What are you here?" It was like I knew what I wanted to say, but it seemed to get lost in translation from my brain to my lips. "You left."

"I did."

I looked around, thinking maybe I had somehow been transported when I fell out the front door. Kind of like Alice in Wonderland, but I was still lying on the floor of my porch. "You're gonna have to explain to me more. You are drunk." I shook my head. "Me." Damn, it was hard to talk.

"You are definitely drunk, babe." The glow from the streetlight barely illuminated Wrecker's face, but a smirk spread across his lips. Such a sexy smirk tucked into his beard. I normally wasn't a beard chick, but there was something about Wrecker's that made me want to reach out and run my fingers through it.

"Why are you here?" I demanded, happy I had managed to talk without sounding drunk.

He stood up and walked the few steps over to me. He crouched down and brushed my hair from my face. "You shouldn't be alone right now."

"Pfft, I'm fine. More than fine, Beardilocks. I am a-okay." I made an "o" with my thumb and pointer finger and looked through the hole at him. "See, so okay I can see you through my hole."

He grabbed my hand and pulled me up off the ground. "What were you doing coming outside? It's half-past two."

I struggled to stand and had to put a hand on his shoulder to keep myself upright. His hand was on my waist, and I leaned into him. "I smoke when I drink. Guess what?" I leaned close to his ear. "I drank."

He mumbled something under his breath, but I realized how close I was to his magnificent beard. My hand itched to reach up and pet him.

Must. Control. Myself.

"That still doesn't explain why you were coming outside."

My hand moved across his shoulder, settling under his chin. "I was going to the tree stump."

"Why?"

I looked up at him. "Because it holds them for me." I looked back at his beard. Oh, fuck it. I was going to touch the damn thing. I combed my fingers through it and sighed. "How is it so soft?"

"What are you doing?"

I shifted my fingers through it and sighed. "Petting you."

"Why?" he demanded.

"Because I can."

He grabbed my hand and pulled it from his beard. "That's it, babe. I'm getting you back into the house and in bed."

"I'm not ready to sleep. I want to smoke, refill my glass, and then watch more cold cases. I think I'm getting really good at solving them even before the police." I looked over my shoulder to the backyard. "As soon as I figure out if I put my cigarettes in that stump, I think I'm going to sign up to be a cold case."

"What in the fuck are you talking about?"

I shook my head. "I meant be the guy who signs cold cases." I patted his shoulder. "You really need to learn how to read between the forgotten words of the drunk." I shakily stood on my tip toes. "I'm the drunk, by the way," I whispered in his ear.

"No shit, babe," he laughed. "If we get these cigarettes then you'll go inside to sleep?"

I nodded. "If by bed you mean drink some more, then yeah, totally. That's what I'm going to do."

"Pipe and Nickel owe me big for this." He swept me up into his arms and clumped down the steps and around the house to the backyard.

"I totally could have walked, you know."

Wrecker turned sideways and ducked under a low-hanging branch. "You don't even have shoes, Alice. How the hell were you going to walk back here?"

I lifted a foot and gasped. Sure as shit, I didn't have shoes on. I wiggled my toes and tapped him on the shoulder.

"I'm holding you, babe. You don't have to tap my shoulder to get my attention."

"What do you think of my nail polish? It's sparkly." I was all over the place. I was worse than a squirrel trying to cross the road.

"Where's the stump?" he demanded.

"It's dark."

"Alice, I'm really trying with you here because you're drunk and going through some shit, but I'm about five minutes away from losing my shit. It's dark because it's two o'clock in the fucking morning and we're trying to find cigarettes you decided to hide in a tree stump."

"When you put it that way, I sound fucking crazy."

He looked down at me.

I squirmed to get out of his arms, and he set me on my feet but held onto my arm. "You could have at least said I'm not crazy," I mumbled. "They're in the little bucket thingy behind the stump."

Wrecker stalked over to the stump, leaned over it, and stood up with the purple bucket in his hand. "This?"

"That's it, unless there happens to be another purple bucket back there."

He pried off the lid, pulled out the baggie that held the last of my cigarettes, and tossed the bucket on the ground. He stalked back to me, bent over, planted his shoulder into my stomach, and lifted me off the ground.

"Hey," I protested. "You need to put the bucket back." I slapped his back and kicked my feet for him to let me down.

He grunted but didn't turn around to fix the bucket. "I'm tired, woman. You're gonna smoke your cigarette, crawl into bed, and then I'm going to pass out on your couch."

"I was with you 'til the couch passing." Couch passing? I was about to start rolling my eyes at myself.

"It's your own damn fault I'm sleeping on the couch. If you hadn't stumbled out of your house, we wouldn't be doing this shit right now."

"I can stumble wherever the hell I want. You are not the boss of me, Beardilocks." I nailed him on the back again. "None of this is my fault. I didn't ask you to come to my bucket, let me pet your beard, and then help me find my cigarette house." I clamped my eyes shut and prayed he wouldn't hear what I had said.

"There is so much wrong in that sentence, I don't even know where to start, woman."

"I much prefer you calling me darlin'."

He climbed the three steps to the porch and charged into the house.

"What about my cigarette?" I yelled. He set me on my feet, and I swayed back and forth.

He dangled the bag in front of my face and rested a hand on my shoulder to steady me. "Smoke, bed."

I snatched the bag from him and took a step back. "I have to go back outside, Beardilocks. I can't smoke in here."

"The fact you can say Beardilocks but can't get a complete sentence out is baffling."

I bowed my head. "You. Are. Welcome."

He grabbed my hand and tugged me back out the front door. "You're a trip, darlin'."

I ignored him and ripped open the baggie. "You wouldn't, by chance, have any fire on you?" He threw his head back and laughed. "I'm not sure on what is so funny."

He patted his pocket, then pulled out my fire I needed. "You mean a lighter?" He flicked the little flicky thing and held it in front of my face.

I stuck the cigarette in my mouth and leaned into the flame. "Lifr eh men." I inhaled deep when the spark caught and leaned back to enjoy the nicotine coursing through me.

"Try that one more time, darlin'."

I exhaled and smiled. "Lighter, I mean."

He nodded but didn't say anything.

We stood there, neither one of us talking, while I smoked my cigarette. I didn't understand how I had gotten there—standing on my front porch with Wrecker after trekking through my backyard to get a damn cigarette.

I tossed the exhausted butt onto the ground, and Wrecker moved to grind it out with his heel. "I didn't know if you were going to remember that you didn't have shoes on."

I glanced down at my feet. "I hadn't." Though it hadn't even registered in my brain to snuff it out. "You can go home now."

He shook his head and grabbed my hand. "No." He tugged me back into the house, past the living room, and down the hallway. "Which one is your bedroom?"

"I'll never tell." There were only two doors so he would shortly figure it out, but I wasn't going to help him.

He opened the one on the left and saw it was the bathroom, then stalked toward the one farther down the hallway. The door was open, and he walked right into my room as if I had invited him.

"Get in bed. I'll be right back." He left as fast as he had walked into my room.

"Do what he says, and then he'll leave," I mumbled. I dropped my shorts, yanked my shirt over my head, and grabbed my pajamas I had left at the foot of my bed. I managed to get them on with only tipping over two times. Go me.

"Take these, drink this, and pass out." Wrecker walked into the room with a huge glass of water and four white pills in his hand. He skidded to a stop in front of me, and some of the water in the glass sloshed onto the floor. "What in the hell are you wearing?"

"Cow print."

He looked me up and down. "Why?"

"Because it's the latest fashion in cow couture, duh."

He looked around the room. "Is this a damn joke?"

"Why would this be a joke? You told me to get ready for bed, and I did." I snatched the pills and water from him.

He motioned to me. "I heard a story about this, but I always thought it was Nickel and Karmen being funny."

I motioned up and down my body. "Does this look like a joke to you?"

"Well, yeah."

I tossed the pills into my mouth, downed half of the water, and thrust the glass into his hand. "You can go."

"Get into bed, and then I'll think about it."

I stomped over to my pillow, yanked back the covers, and bounced into the bed. "You know, you telling me to get into bed should be sexy, but all I want to do right now is punch you in the nuts."

He walked over to the door and flipped off the lights. "Night, babe." He pulled the door halfway shut, and I listened to his footfalls down the hallway.

"What in the blooming hell just happened?" I whispered.

This had to be a dream. Or I was so wasted that I was hallucinating the big, burly, hunk of man in my house. That had to be what was happening.

I laid back and pulled the covers up to my chin. Too bad I hadn't hallucinated the man falling into bed with me. That would have been *awesome*. There had been more than a handful of times I had imagined what it would feel like to have his beard against my skin.

If what I felt tonight when I ran my fingers through it was any indication, I knew if I ever managed to get his beard to touch other parts of me, it would be better than pigs rolling in mud. I closed my eyes and tried to squelch a wave of nausea.

Jesus. I hadn't planned on drinking that much but the more I drank, the less I thought about my mom. My brain had become foggy, and I didn't remember I was basically all alone in the world now. Except now that I was lying in the dark, nauseous, with the feeling of floating, the tears soaked my cheeks again.

Drunk or not, I was alone.

*

CHAPTER 2

WRECKER

I had slept on some shitty couches in my day, but Alice's piece of shit took the cake. Springs digging into my back and the huge gap between two of the cushions made for a shit night of sleep. It was only six thirty, and I was already up because my body decided if it couldn't get comfortable then we might as well be awake.

"Fuck." I tossed the tiny as fuck blanket to the side and jack-knifed off the couch. It had only been three hours since I put Alice to bed, and thankfully, I hadn't heard a sound from her room since.

I crept down the hallway, pushed open the door, and couldn't help but laugh. When I left, she had been sitting on the bed, but now, she was hanging half off with her feet touching the floor and her head in middle. Her mouth was hanging wide open, and her hair was fanned out in a wild and snarly mess. Even in her sleep, she was crazy.

She was totally going to wake up with a wicked headache and a sore back. I moved into the room. I couldn't do anything about the headache, but I could try to help her back. I slid my arm under her legs to swing them up onto the bed, but as soon as I moved her, she bent her knees, trapping my arm and twisted up onto the bed. She yanked me up and onto the bed with my arm trapped as she continued to snore lightly.

"Son of a bitch," I whispered to the dark room. *What the fuck am I supposed to do now?* I tried to wiggle my way out from under her, but she clamped her legs even harder to her ass. Now I was the one who was half lying on the bed with my feet on the floor. I was twisted into a pretzel with Alice, and I had no fucking clue how to get out of it without waking her up.

She muttered in her sleep, something along the lines of butterflies and peanut butter then settled back into snoring with a death clamp on my arm.

Her sweet scent clung to the sheets, and I buried my face in them for a brief second. Her bed was soft as fuck compared to the shitass couch I had tried sleeping on. My fatigue from riding hard yesterday to get back to the club and then making a stop at her house which kept me up 'til almost three in the morning, hit me hard.

I wrapped my other arm around her waist, moved her further to the side of the bed, and managed to get my whole body onto the mattress. Through all of this, she didn't wake up or release her damn legs from my arm. I twisted to grab a pillow and shoved it under my head.

Not how I had expected this to go, but at least I had a better place to sleep now. She must have found the couch in a dumpster and spent a pretty penny on her bed. It was like I was lying on a fucking cloud.

She was going to freak the fuck out when she woke up and saw me sleeping here, but it was her own damn fault.

*

ALICE

Oh fuck. What have you done, Alice? I looked over at the pillow by my ass and saw Wrecker's bearded face and felt his body wrapped around me. "Holy shit." It hadn't been a hallucination last night. Although, when I fell asleep, Wrecker had been in the living room, or at least, that was where he was headed.

How in the facking hell did he end up in my bed? I needed to get out of there fast. The clock on my nightstand glowed that it was half-past nine, and a fire lit under my ass when I realized I had to be to work in half an hour.

Double oh fuck.

I slid out from his hold and scrambled off the bed without waking him up. It was amazing the ninja skills I had when trying not to wake a sleeping giant on my bed. I sprinted to the bathroom and quietly clicked the door shut behind me.

I looked in the mirror and clamped my hand over my mouth to muffle my scream. "You're hideous, Alice," I whispered. The mascara and eyeliner I had swiped on yesterday was now smeared down my face; the eyeshadow had somehow blended to cover all the way up to my eyebrows; and it looked like I was a raccoon with a rat's nest of burgundy hair.

"Sweet creamy peanut butter." I patted my hair, hoping to somehow tap it into submission. It was going to take a whole hell of a lot more than a brush to look presentable in twenty minutes.

After I reached into the shower to twist the faucet to scalding hot, I unzipped my onesie, dropped it to the floor, and stepped out of it. Thank God, I had bought the industrial size of conditioner because that shit was about to become my detangler.

It took five minutes of standing under the steamy water massaging gobs of conditioner in my hair to finally be able to run my hands through it without thinking I was going to lose a finger.

I peeked my head out of the shower curtain after rinsing off to listen for Wrecker moving around. I heard nothing and said a silent prayer thanking God for the small miracle of keeping that man asleep.

My daily routine of hanging my work uniform on the back of the bathroom door saved me from having to go back into the bedroom. I was dressed and out of the bathroom with one minute to spare before I needed to be in the car.

I popped a pod into the coffee machine, stuck a travel cup under it, and gave it the stink eye when it made a hissing noise that was loud enough to wake up the neighbors. I snapped on the lid, grabbed my purse, and hightailed it out the front door.

Dealing with Wrecker was a little foggy in my mind, but I knew I had made a fool of myself. Normally, I was fine with making a fool of myself because that was who I was, but when it came to Wrecker, I couldn't handle the man's judgy eyes. Reliving that humiliation was not something I wanted to do.

"Mother flappers!" He had parked behind my car. "Argh!"

How the hell was I going to get out of here without waking him up now? It was like he had purposely parked there.

"I hate him. It's official." I walked to the front of the car and saw I had about five feet from the bumper to the garage. If I managed to back up a bit and then crank my wheel, I should be able to get out. I would have to drive on the lawn, but at that point, I would have driven through two feet of water if it meant I didn't have to wake up Wrecker.

After I managed to eke out of my driveway with only tipping over a flower pot and thankfully, not Wrecker's bike, I motored down the road while glancing in my rearview mirror the whole time to make sure Wrecker somehow didn't appear behind me.

"Just in time," Bos shouted from the kitchen.

I rolled my eyes and stowed my purse under the counter. "You got three people in here, Bos. Not like you were swamped."

He leaned on the window that separated the kitchen and the front of the diner. "You know I'm going to have to hire another waitress to replace Nikki."

I waved my hand. "Go ahead. I don't know what's stopping you."

"It'll give you more time to spend with your mom."

I crouched down and grabbed a stack of paper placemats. "Yeah, that would be good." Tears stung my eyes, but I fought them off. Bos didn't know Mom had died. No one knew besides the pastor and the nursing home she lived in two towns over. News would eventually spread that she had died, but I didn't know how to say she was gone without making people feel sorry for me.

"Alice, can I get a refill?"

Saved by asshole Phil needing a refill every two minutes. "I'll get that," I mumbled. I grabbed the coffee pot but not without noticing Bos assessing me.

He was another one who I knew was always watching me. He wasn't really judging, but he seemed to know what was going on without asking any questions. Not like he could know my mom had died, but I could tell he knew something was up. Time to lay on the normal crazy Alice to throw him off whatever scent he was on.

"You think you can toast me up three pieces of toast, smear 'em with peanut butter, and toss two fried eggs on top?"

He wrinkled his nose in disgust. "Don't know how the hell you manage to eat shit like that."

I shrugged and made my way over to Phil. "It tastes good, Bos. You should try it sometime." I filled Phil's coffee and listened to him ramble on about the prices of wheat then wandered back over to the front counter where I mindlessly started slapping a Diner sticker on all the paper placemats. This was how cheap Bos was. Instead of just getting the damn mats with the Diner logo on them, he ordered them separate because it was cheaper and then made me slap them together. "Cheap ass," I mumbled.

"What was that?" He smacked the bell in the window and clattered down the plate with my breakfast.

I finished the mats and set two at the places at the counter. "Oh nothing, Bos. I was just thinking about how much I love all of these tasks that you give me. Keeps me busy." I grabbed my plate from the window and a set of silverware wrapped in a napkin from the bin under the counter.

"You better refill Phil before you sit down," Bos warned.

"Can I get a refill?"

I rolled my eyes and set my plate down. "Coming, Phil." I could already tell it was going to be a day of endless refills for Phil and Bos being his annoying self.

Yippee.

*

CHAPTER 3

WRECKER

"What are you doing?"

"Making a bowl of ice cream."

I glanced at the clock above the stove. "It's fucking ten thirty in the morning, Boink."

"Not sure what your point is, Wrecker, but I don't like what your tone is intending."

Dumbass. "Well, when you are done eating your ice cream, I need you to pack."

"For what?" he mumbled.

"Can you please wait 'til I'm off the fucking phone before you start shoveling your face full?"

He gulped loud and belched. "Only for you, bossman."

I rolled my eyes. Boink was a fucking idiot. He was never serious and always shoving his face full of food no matter when he had eaten. "Pack."

"For how long?"

"Pack enough shit for a week. You'll be there longer than that, though."

"Where the hell am I going? You shipping me off to summer camp?" he chuckled.

"If summer camp is watching The Ultra for the next few weeks while I get some personal shit ironed out, then yeah. It's fucking summer camp, Boink." I was dealing with idiots. Each day, it was like I was trying to herd cats into a box. Except they kept tipping the fucking thing over and coming home with female cats to add to the fucking chaos.

"What personal stuff are you dealing with?"

I grabbed my cup of coffee from under the maker and blew on it. "Personal, Boink."

He aahed. "I get ya."

He didn't get me, but I wasn't going to say anything. "I'll be back to the club in a couple of hours."

"Where are you?"

I wasn't going to do this. No one asked me where I was or what I was doing. "Personal."

"Damn, brother. You on the rag or some shit?"

"Be ready when I get there. If you're not, I'm going to kick your ass." I ended the call and tossed the phone on the counter.

I was still at Alice's. After I woke up alone and saw her car was gone, I made a cup of coffee and called Boink.

Last night, before I fell asleep, I started to form a plan in my head. Boink was going to have to start taking a little bit more responsibility in the club. I had been spending most of my time watching Raven while she infiltrated The Ultra, but now, something more important had come up.

My phone dinged, and I hoped it was Pipe with an answer to my question.

The Diner. Five blocks from her house on West St.

I fired off a quick thank you. Pipe knew how I operated. He knew if I was asking a question, all I wanted was the answer and not a question about why I was asking it.

Alice was gone, but I figured she was at work. On my way out of town, I planned on taking a little drive past the diner to make sure she was there before I headed back to Weston. I would be back before nightfall, but I wanted to be sure she was fine until then.

Since she so rudely left me without a goodbye this morning, I helped myself to her coffee and leaned against the counter.

There was more going on with Alice. She may act all goofy as shit and wear weird as fuck clothes, but it was all a cover. A cover for what, I wasn't sure.

"Fuck." Maybe I was wrong. Maybe she was just goofy as shit and that was it. I had only spent barely an hour with her plastered to my back when I gave her a motorcycle ride a couple months back, and she hadn't spoken much then except for the occasional gasp and startled cry when I gunned the engine.

I dumped the rest of the coffee down the sink. I needed to get out of here and feel my tires hit the pavement. I did my best thinking when there wasn't anything between me and the open road.

I shoved my phone in my back pocket, grabbed my cut off the back of the kitchen chair, and headed out the front door. I threaded my arms through the holes, locked the door behind me with the spare key I had dug out of her massive junk drawer, and threw a leg over my bike.

She had somehow managed to maneuver her car out from in front of my bike, which was surprising. I glanced at the flower pot that was tipped over and split down the side. She obviously hadn't made it out smoothly, but she had made it out.

I backed my bike around so I was facing the road and fired it up. The motor rumbled beneath me, and a peace settle over me that I only felt when I was riding.

Shit with Alice was fucked up, but I was going to figure out what the hell was going on. Hopefully, it wasn't going to take that long, but I was prepared for however long it took.

*

CHAPTER 4

ALICE

"Why the heck didn't you answer the phone yesterday? Or the two days before that?"

Because my mother was dying, and then I was trying to bury her. I cradled the phone between my ear and shoulder. "Um, I was just really tired. I slept most of the day." I jabbed the key into the lock and pushed the door open with my foot.

"Karmen had the baby."

"Shut up," I gasped.

"Nope. We were drinking and then it happened."

"I hope you *all* weren't drinking."

Nikki scoffed. "Of course, Karmen wasn't. Cora and I were drinking her share."

"Well, spill the details, woman." I closed the door and tossed my purse on the couch.

"Baby Cole came blazing into the world three days ago, weighing in at a whopping nine pounds, seven ounces."

"Holy cannoli, that's a big baby. She push it out on her own?" I kicked off my shoes and padded into the kitchen in search of what I had been looking forward to my whole shift.

"Oh, yeah. When I say he came screaming into this world, I actually mean the screaming came from Karmen."

I chuckled and reached into the freezer to pull out a large bottle of vodka. "I bet she wished she was drinking when she went into labor."

"She did ask for a bottle of rum to activate her inner pirate halfway through. I think that was the first time Nickel had actually said no to her."

"How did that go?"

"She screamed. More."

I reached into the cabinet, pulled out a glass, and dropped a few ice cubes from the freezer in it.

"What are you doing?"

"Uh, getting a glass of water." I grabbed the pitcher of orange juice from the fridge and filled the glass halfway.

"You're better than I am. I already had a pineapple with rum, and Pipe is making me another one."

"Such a good little biker," I chuckled.

She cleared her throat. "So, did you have a visitor last night?"

I rolled my eyes. Her laugh tinkled through the phone, and I twisted the cap off the bottle of vodka. "Yes."

"Annnd?" she drawled.

"And he was here, and then he left." I filled the glass to the rim and set the bottle on the counter.

"That's it?"

"Yeah, that was it, Nikki." I wasn't going to tell her anything more than the bare minimum facts.

She huffed. "Well, that wasn't the excitement I thought you were going to tell me. So, when are you going to come visit baby Cole and me?"

"Um, I have to work the next few days. Hopefully soon."

I could hear her roll her eyes through the phone. "Girl, don't let Bos work you to the bone. He needs to get someone in there to replace me. It's been over two months."

"We had Mariah for a bit. Or was it Michele?"

"The fact you can't even remember her name just goes to show how shitty she was."

"That's because no one can replace you, Nikki." We went around on this every time we talked. I worked too much. Bos needed to get off his ass and hire someone. Blah, blah, blah. Normally, she was pacified by me saying she was irreplaceable.

"You're right, but Bos is going to have to try a little harder to get someone to help you."

I grabbed my glass and plopped down on the couch. "I'll tell him that tomorrow morning." I took a sip. The cool concoction slid down my throat, and I welcomed its numbing effects.

"Why don't you come down this weekend?"

"I'll try."

"I want you to do more than try."

If I went, there was a possibility I would see Wrecker. The same man who I was ninety-nine percent sure I had made a fool of myself in front of. "If I'm not working, I'll be there." I was going to beg Bos to let me work.

"If not, I'll send Wrecker after you again."

Ha. I was going to keep the door locked and barred the whole weekend. "I'll see what I can swing, Nikki. If I can't, maybe Pipe and Nickel will let you and Karmen come for a visit."

She blew a raspberry into the phone. "You know Nickel isn't letting Karmen out of his sight. She popped that baby out three days ago."

"We do have a hospital if anything would happen." It was a small one, but we had one.

"Kales Corners could have a state of the art, best hospital in the world, and he still wouldn't let her or Cole out of his sight." Pipe yelled for her in the background. "I gots ta run. My biker man is calling me. I'll see you this weekend."

"I never pro—" The line went dead before I could remind her that I made no promises to come to Weston this weekend.

I wanted to see Cole, but if I was being a truthful jealous bitch, I didn't want to. I didn't want to do a damn thing besides drink what was in my glass and then drink two more just like it as soon as it was empty.

Those were the only plans I had for the next few days and the weekend.

Work.
Get Drunk.
Repeat.
Starting right now.

*

CHAPTER 5

WRECKER

All the lights were on.

I had planned on getting a hotel room for the night since it was much later than I intended on rolling into town, but when I drove past Alice's house, I stopped. The house was lit up like a Christmas tree so I decided, since it looked like she was still awake, I would stop to check in on her. I knew she wasn't going to be happy to see me, but she was going to have to deal with it.

I stayed on my bike, watching the front window.

She was dancing.

Or having a seizure.

It was hard to tell, but from the sound of music coming from the house, I figured it was dancing. Bad dancing, but still dancing.

I lit the cigarette hanging from the corner of my mouth and inhaled.

She was drunk again. A glass hung from her fingertips as she spun around recklessly. She took a long drink from it then spun around again before banging into the coffee table. She hopped around holding her shin and yelled at the table.

She was crazy.

I took one last drag, tossed the butt onto the driveway, and ground it out with my heel as I swung off the bike.

The music faded in the house as I climbed the steps and knocked on the front door.

Alice swung the door open and leaned heavily against it. "Wrecker, how are you delivering pizza on your bikey?"

"Bikey?"

She nodded her head in the direction of the driveway. "Yea. Did you put a basket on the front?" She pushed past me and stumbled onto the porch. "I wanna see the basket. You should put streamers on the handlebars too."

I grabbed her arm and yanked her back into the house. "Woman, where in the hell do you think you are going?"

"Oh!" she yelled. "You should put the cards in your spokes." She waved her hand in my face. "That way it'll make like…a…" She made a farting noise and sputtered, peppering my face with spit. "I bet I've got a deck of cards in the kitchen," she slurred, unaware she had spit all over me.

I raked a hand down my face and wiped it on my pants. "It's a motorcycle, Alice. Not a *bikey*."

She laid a hand on my shoulder and leaned into me. "What I really need to know is if you brought the pizza and if you want my deck of cards to make the—"

She pursed her lips to blow another raspberry, and I laid my hand over her mouth before she wound up and let her spit fly again.

"No pizza, and I don't need your cards."

She slapped my shoulder. "Well, thank God I didn't give you a tip. You didn't even bring the pizza, Beardilocks." She threaded her fingers through my beard and sighed. "I bet you condition this."

I hooked a finger under her chin and tilted her head back to look me in the eye. "How wasted are you, babe?"

A goofy smile spread across her lips. "How did you know?" she gushed.

I would have to say she was completely wasted. "Did you order pizza?" For all I knew, she was just craving pizza and thought about ordering it but never did.

"Yeah. Talked to Jim. Or is it Tim?" She touched a finger to her nose. "Marco."

It was half-past ten. I doubted there was pizza delivery in Kales Corners after seven o'clock at night, let alone almost eleven. "How long ago did you order?"

She hummed and squeezed the tip of her nose. "If I were to look at the wall, I would have to say at least a minute ago." She shook her head. "I mean an hour ago." A crazy giggle erupted from her lips.

"What's so funny?"

"You're here again. I should put a bell on you."

I couldn't keep up with her drunken thoughts. From tricking out my bike, to pizza, conditioning my beard, and then back to pizza in less than two minutes was more than I could handle. "Why don't you sit down, and I'll figure out where the pizza is."

"It's with Jim-Timmy-Marco."

I guided her over to the couch and helped her sit down.

She motioned for me to come closer.

I crouched down.

"Can I tell you something?"

I nodded and hoped she wasn't about to change the topic drastically.

She sobered and tilted her head to the side. "My momma was the best person I ever knew. She loved me no matter what."

"Is that so?"

She nodded. "Even when I got stuck in the cornfield over on Grim Road with Mark Allen locked in my trunk." She sniffled and wiped her nose with the back of her hand. "As soon as we got him out of the trunk and he dropped the charges, Momma told me she loved me."

That was where the problem came in with Alice being so wasted. I had no idea if what she was saying was true or was the alcohol talking. I wanted to believe the whole trunk thing had to be the multiple drinks she had talking, but the way she told the story so matter-of-factly made me think she was telling the story right. "Now, that is a good mom, babe."

A sad smile spread across her lips. "She was the best, Wrecker."

"I wish I could have met her."

"Me too," she whispered. She closed her eyes and leaned back into the couch. "Can you get me pizza, Wrecker?" And now she was back on wanting pizza.

"Is that what you really want, babe?"

She nodded. "You can't give me what I really want so I guess pizza will have to do," she whispered.

I patted her leg and stood up. "Pizza coming up, babe. You want me to put a movie on for you?"

She opened her eyes and yanked a throw pillow from under her ass. "Yeah. I wanna watch *Back to the Future*. The third one. I don't like the second one. Marty is sexy in the third one." She fell on her side and shoved the pillow under her head. "I like one, though."

I couldn't keep up with her random and wandering thoughts. My goal was to get her fed, have her swallow some painkillers, and hope she passed out during the movie.

It took ten minutes to find the damn movie she wanted to watch. The opening credits of the movie rolled as I walked into the kitchen and tried to figure out what I was going to do about pizza.

After two phone calls to the local pizza places, I was onto plan B of praying she had some frozen pizza. Luckily, when I opened the large chest freezer she had tucked in the corner by the patio door, there was a treasure trove of every pizza under the sun.

I grabbed a sausage and pepperoni pizza that boasted it was thick crust in big, bold letters. She drank a shit-ton if the more than half empty bottle was any indication. Thick, bready crust was good to help soak up all the vodka.

"Wrecker?" she called warily.

"Yeah, babe?"

"Oh, I thought you left," she said quietly.

"Not leaving. Just getting your pizza going." I cranked on the oven, unwrapped the pizza, and set it on the middle rack. "Fifteen minutes and it's all yours."

"Can you bring me my drink? I can't remember where I left it."

I opened the fridge and spotted a bottle of sweet tea. "How about some tea?" I glanced in the living room to see her wrinkle her nose in disgust.

"Uh, I said my drink."

"I think you had enough of that drink. Why don't you try something new?"

"Can you make the drink that turns Karmen into a pirate?"

Jesus. "I'll make you something special, how about that?" It wasn't going to be any pirate punch shit she wanted.

"A Wrecker Special?" she called.

It was a damn good thing no one else was here, and I was pretty sure Alice wasn't going to remember any of this come morning. If one of the guys from the club would have heard her say Wrecker Special, the jokes would have been endless. I grabbed the sweet tea, a jar of maraschino cherries, and an orange from the fridge. "One Wrecker Special coming right up."

I filled a glass with sweet tea, added a splash of cherry juice, dropped three cherries in, and garnished it with a wedge of orange. I held it up and nodded. It looked like a mixed drink, and Alice was so far gone, she wasn't going to even realize she was just drinking tea.

"Here ya go, babe." I set the drink on the coffee table in front of her.

"You made that for me?"

"You asked for a Wrecker Special." If anyone would have heard those words come out of my mouth, they would have thought I was being held at gunpoint.

She sat up and grabbed the glass. "Oh, you added cherries. Cherries make everything better." She took a hesitant sip and smiled. "That is super good, Wrecker. You should give everyone the Wrecker Special."

Jesus. It was like she didn't have a filter from her brain to her mouth. If she thought it, she was going to say it.

She laid back down, her eyes trained on the TV. "Did Nickel and Pipe send you here again to check on me?"

"Nobody sends me to do anything."

She glanced up at me. "Is that so?" She looked back at the TV.

I didn't answer.

"Oh-kay," she sang. "Then why are you here again?"

"Thought you might need some company." A simple answer.

One she thankfully bought. "Company is good sometimes." She looked up at me. "Are you going to stand there all night looking at me?"

"Just making sure you're good."

She hiccuped and tucked her legs to her butt. "Is anyone ever really good?"

She looked so tiny and frail lying on the couch. One minute, she was happy-go-lucky Alice, and the next, she transformed into a shell of the person she normally was. It was fucking trippy, and I didn't like it at all.

The oven timer buzzed, interrupting my thought. "Still hungry?"

She scoffed. "Does a bear shit in the woods?"

I laughed and walked into the kitchen. "Hang tight, babe. Pizza coming up." I didn't know how to help Alice just yet, but I could at least give her the things she was actually asking for.

Pizza and *Back to the Future* were what she was getting tonight. She was going to need a whole fuck of a lot more than that, though.

*

CHAPTER 6

ALICE

It happened again.

I don't know how it did, but it did.

I got drunk and woke up to Wrecker in my house.

It was like he had some drunk radar. It was like the bat signal, but instead of signaling bad guys doing shit, it signaled to him that I was tanked.

At least this morning he wasn't in bed with me. Instead, he was sleeping on my couch, and I felt rather sorry for him. My couch sucked.

It had been my mom's couch, but it still sucked. The only reason I had it was because it had lived in her house for over twenty years. That was why the cushions were so worn and random springs poked and prodded you when you sat on it. I was used to it, but there was no way in hell Wrecker could be.

It was half-past eight, and I should have been getting ready for work, but instead, I was standing over Wrecker, watching him breath.

If you would have told me watching someone sleep was fascinating, I would have asked what the hell you were smoking, but yet, there I stood, unable to take my eyes off the man.

His eyes popped open, and I jumped back. My calves bumped into the coffee table, and I struggled to keep my balance. I was hung over with a whole ton of wobbliness still affecting me. "What the hell, man?" I gasped. Who in the hell wakes up like that? Dead sleep, and then suddenly he was wide awake.

"You were watching me."

Uh, yeah. But his damn eyes had been closed, and as far as I could tell, he was sleeping. "No, I wasn't." Deny, deny, deny.

"Then what the hell are you doing standing over me?"

"I'm not standing over you," I scoffed.

"Alice."

"Wrecker."

"Are you still drunk?"

"What?" I scoffed. "Of course not." Maybe just a little.

"Then you wanna take a step to the right so I can stand up?"

"You don't need to get up. I'm just going to go to work." I wasn't going to be able to function with him moving around while I tried to shower and get dressed.

"Babe. I gotta take a leak."

I wrinkled my nose and moved to the side of the couch. "Classy."

He rolled his eyes and swung his legs off the couch. "I'm the president of a motorcycle club. Classy isn't in my vocabulary." He jack-knifed off the couch and stood toe to toe with me.

"Huh, hi." My eyes were glued to his feet. Seeing Wrecker with no burly boots on was straight-up weird. "You have feet." *Shoot. Me. Now.*

He looked down. "Yeah. So do you, babe."

"I meant it's weird that you have feet." My God. The stupid just kept falling out of my mouth.

"Not sure what you thought I had other than feet," he drawled.

"I just meant, I never thought of you having feet."

We both raised our heads, and he quirked an eyebrow. "Not sure what you thought I would have other than feet," he repeated.

"I really don't have an answer to that question without sounding like a complete idiot." Laying it all out there. The man had to have figured out by now that I was weird in so many ways. It was normally just best to accept I was crazy and go with the flow.

"Has that ever stopped you before?" A smirk spread across his lips, and there was a twinkle in his eye.

Was Wrecker flirting with me? Or at the very least, being nice to me? I was used to surly, rough man who barely spoke, but when he did, you listened. This was new, and to be honest, it completely threw me off my game. "Normally no, but with you, I have no idea what to say."

"I'd ask why that is, but I'm sure you'd start rambling about cows and the price of popcorn."

"Popcorn?" I laughed. "I think my randomness might be rubbing off on you."

He brushed my hair behind my ear. "Doubtful, babe. I just know to expect random shit from you."

Was I supposed to be flattered? "Can we get back to why you are here?"

"As soon as we talk about why you were standing over me while I slept."

Pfft, like that was going to happen. "I need to shower."

"That's what I thought."

"I'm not sure I like your tone."

He leaned in and rested a hand on my hip. "I'm not sure I care if you like it or not."

My jaw dropped. "You're an ass."

"Been called worse, babe. Let me hit the john and then it's all yours." He headed down the hallway before I could sputter out a reply.

He wasn't even gone a minute before he walked back into the living room. "All yours, babe." He walked into the kitchen as if he lived here and grabbed a coffee pod from the bin next to the Keurig.

"What's happening?" I whispered.

Wrecker popped the pod in and snapped the lid shut. He turned around, leaned on the counter, and crossed his arms over his chest. "I'm making you a cup of coffee; you're jumping in the shower; and then, we both have to get to work."

I shook my head. "Let's start at the beginni—"

"Babe. We ain't got time to go over whatever the hell is going on in your head. You need to be to work in twenty minutes, and I got a two-hour ride back to the clubhouse."

I glanced at the clock on the stove. He was right. I didn't have time to stand around and argue with him. I pointed a finger at him. "I'm only going to take a shower because I can't be late for work. Not because that is what you decided we were going to do."

He held up his hands. "Whatever you say."

I humphed, knowing he was only patronizing me. After I stomped down the hallway to the bathroom, I slammed the door shut and let out a frustrated scream. Things were happening, and I had absolutely no freaking control over them.

A week ago, I had no one besides my mom. Now, my mom was gone and Wrecker was here. "I'd like a trade." Send Wrecker back to Weston and give me back my mom.

I closed my eyes and shook my head. "If only it were that easy."

Mom was gone, and Wrecker kept popping up like a damn pimple on prom night.

It was time to pop that sucker and get rid of him. Wrecker needed to go away, and I was going to do everything I could to make sure he did.

*

"Bye." Alice ducked into her car and slammed the door shut.

I walked over to her door, rapped on the window, and crossed my arms over my chest.

She started the car and looked up at me but didn't roll down the window.

I reached for the door handle, but she locked the door before I could tug it open.

"What do you want?" she shouted through the glass.

"For you to open the damn window."

She shook her head. "Remember? I have to get to work."

"You flip your bitch switch on, babe?"

Her jaw dropped, and it looked like her head was either going to explode or she was going to punch me in the junk. She rolled down the window with a death glare. "You did not just say that."

I had. Wasn't going to deny it. "Not sure what happened from talking to you in the living room to now, where you won't even look at me."

"I'm looking at you, Wrecker," she ground out between clenched teeth.

I draped my forearm above her door and leaned into her window. "No, babe. You aren't looking at me. Not how you should be."

She rolled her eyes and shifted into reverse. "There's only one way to look at you, Wrecker, with my eyes."

I shook my head. "Not what I mean, but I don't think you're ready to have that discussion."

"Good. Now move away from my car before I run over your foot."

A chuckle rumbled from my throat. "Is that a threat?"

"A warning," she replied sweetly.

"What time are you going to be home?"

"I won't be to *my* home until late. I have plans after work."

What the hell was there to do in this town? "What time are you going to be home?"

She growled and plastered a fake smile on her face. "I'm not sure, Wrecker. But the last time I checked, you aren't my father so I don't really need to check in with you. Get on your bike and drive away."

"Planned on it. Got some things going on with the club." Though I think she meant she didn't want me to come back.

"Cool. Have a nice life, Wrecker." She rolled up her window with a jaunty little wave and backed out of the driveway.

I watched her drive away and noticed she had her license plate personalized with "craycray." "At least she embraces it," I muttered.

My phone vibrated in my pocket. I pulled it out to see Boink had texted me.

What the hell did you get me into?

Boink must have met Raven. **What's wrong?**

There's too much to fuxing type.

Jesus Christ. All he had to do was keep an eye on Raven and make sure she didn't get in too deep with The Ultra. What was so fucking hard about that? I connected the call to him and put the phone to my ear.

"How the hell do I keep an eye on someone that I don't even know who they are?"

I walked back onto the porch and sat down on the rocking chair. "I told you she works at Sparky's."

He scoffed in my ear. "Because there is only one chick that works here, right? Jesus, Wrecker."

"Look at the damn name tags."

"I tried that last night. There are four fucking Raven's that work there. Four!" he yelled. "How does that even happen?"

Probably because most of the girls who work there didn't use their real name. Raven was probably the only one whose real name was actually that. "Long black hair. White as fuck skin. Talking ghost-like skin. Looks like she could rip your balls off with one look." The Raven I wanted him to watch was hard to miss.

"Now why the hell couldn't you have told me that yesterday? Would have saved me a ton of running after four chicks yesterday."

Fuck, Boink drove me insane. "Why didn't you call and ask me when you were there?"

"'Cause you said you were dealing with personal shit, and I didn't want to interrupt."

All he would have interrupted was me making Alice a damn pizza. "Was that the only problem you had?" I seriously had given him one task. Watch Raven when she was working. Didn't even need to talk to her if he didn't want to. She was still trying to gain the trust of Oakley Mykel. It had been slow going, but Oakley was starting to notice her.

"Aren't they going to notice me there all the time?"

"Well, if you make it fucking obvious what you are doing, then yeah, they are going to figure you out." Did I really have to do everything?

"So just look like a local drunk going to the bar every night."

"Yes. Exactly." It really shouldn't be that far a stretch for him. "Just watch her 'til I get my shit figured out here."

He cleared his throat. "And just where is exactly is *here*?"

"Where I am."

"How is it you can disappear without anyone knowing where you are, but we can't take a piss without you knowing?"

"'Cause I'm the prez, that's why. As soon as one of you dipshits decides that they can do my job, I'll gladly hand over the reins. I might like just having to do one thing and not have to worry about all the shit that keeps the club going."

Boink grumbled but didn't say he wanted prez. "All right, all right. I get your point."

"Any other questions? Or can I get on with the rest of my day now?" I was pissed. Questioning me on my shit was a sure-fire way to piss me off and maybe get your ass kicked. It was a good thing for Boink he wasn't here.

"Ah, no. That's all."

"Good. Figure out which one Raven is, keep your damn eye on her, and make sure nothing happens to her."

"Wait. I do have one question."

Fuck me running. "Yeah?"

"What do I do if something happens?"

"You fucking protect her, Boink. Protect. Her." I jabbed my finger at the end call button and shoved it in my pocket.

Was what I wanted him to do really that fucking hard? Raven had the shit job of trying to get in with Oakley. All Boink had to do was watch her and drink beer her whole shift. The bonehead somehow had questions on how to do that.

I needed to get to the clubhouse for church today. Most of the guys were wondering what was going on, and I had gone as far as I could with keeping them in the dark. Dealing with The Ultra was like nothing we had ever done before.

They were a well-oiled machine of crime that could easily wipe the Fallen Lords MC off the map if they felt like it. The same went with Raven. At the end of the day, she was just a woman to Oakley who could easily be replaced if she didn't play her cards right.

I was banking on Oakley falling for Raven and her giving us an in to have Oakley realize the mess Jenkins had made had nothing to do with the Weston chapter. No one got to Oakley by just walking off the street to talk to him. Raven was my plan, and it was going to have to fucking work.

I had planned on taking care of everything myself, but I couldn't be in two places at once, and I felt that I needed to be here more than there. I was one of those suckers I always made fun of. Alice drew me to her, and I couldn't just walk away knowing what I did or what I thought I knew. She was drowning. I saw it each time when she opened the door to me. She couldn't hide it away behind her craziness before I saw it.

Alice was headed down a dangerous path. A path those who followed down didn't come back the same person. If they even made it back at all.

She was lost and trying to find her way in the bottom of a bottle, and I was going to be the one to help her find the way out.

*

CHAPTER 7

ALICE

"You wanna go out tonight?"

Bos looked up from the grill. "I know you ain't talking to me, girl."

I looked around the deserted restaurant. "Well, you're the only one here, so yes, I'm talking to you."

"Don't you got some Girl Gang you should be hanging out with? Last I checked, you and I didn't hang out unless I was standing in front of a hot ass grill and you were slinging coffee."

That was true, but I didn't want to go home. "Then I think we are overdue to hang out. We should get to know each other better."

Bos looked at me like I had sprouted wings. "Are you feeling okay?"

No, I wasn't. I could feel the loneliness creeping in, and I didn't want to deal with it at that moment. If I was with people, I wouldn't feel alone, right? That was why I was begging Bos to hang out with me. "Nothing a beer and a game of pool won't fix. Just come to The Bar with me for one drink, Bos." Or ten beers.

"I had plans with Mazie tonight."

"Then bring her along! The more, the merrier."

He wearily leaned against the grill. "If I agree to go, then you have to clean the grill and the deep fryer tomorrow."

Damn, he drove a hard bargain. "Yes, to the grill, but no to the fryer." Cleaning the grill sucked monster donkey balls. I wasn't into donkey balls.

He shook his head. "Sorry, doll. But if you want me going out with you tonight, that is the only way it's going to happen."

I could just go to The Bar myself. There had to be someone there I could hang with. Although, there could also be people there I didn't want to hang out with. At least if I brought Bos, I could ignore them since I had someone else to talk to. I stuck my hand through the window pass. "Fine, you have a deal. But I'm not happy about your trickery and demands."

He shook my hand and grinned. "Glad to see we could come to an agreement."

"The fact I have to do your dirty work in order for you to hang out with me doesn't bode well for our blossoming friendship."

He shrugged. "I don't see a problem with it from where I'm standing."

I grabbed my rag off the counter. "Well, maybe you'll have a problem with it when you're the one having to walk me home tonight."

"Hey, I never signed up for being your designated walker."

"Eh." I shrugged and walked to the far end of the diner to start wiping down all the tables. "Make sure you have your walking shoes on, Bos."

He grumbled but didn't back out of our deal.

I wiped the first table then called to Bos. "Do we have a blender I can borrow for the night? The one in my trunk busted."

*

WRECKER

"When you gonna be back?"

I swung my leg over my bike and looked back at Pipe and Maniac. "Not sure. Probably a few days." It was Thursday, and while I loved being on the bike, driving back and forth to Weston every day wasn't something I wanted to do. Especially when I didn't start the drive back to Kales Corners 'til after seven. I wouldn't be back to Alice 'til after nine, and I knew she was going to be halfway in the bag by the time I knocked on the door.

Though she had told me she had plans tonight and wasn't going to be home.

"You're really not gonna tell us what the hell you are up to?" Pipe asked.

"Hadn't planned on it, but you might be able to help me with something, Pipe." I didn't like to ask for help, but if Pipe gave me some information about Kales Corners, it would cut down on the time I would waste looking for Alice if she wasn't home.

"What do you need?" he asked.

"What is there to do in Kales Corners?"

His brow furrowed, and his jaw dropped.

Maniac laughed and shook his head. "Fucking knew it when I heard you went to check on Alice."

"Knew what?" I growled.

"That you were going to fall for her crazy ass."

"I didn't fall for anyone." I hadn't been able to hit Boink when he was giving me shit on the phone before, but now it looked like Maniac was going to be on the receiving end of my fist.

"Well, you at least fell into bed with her and can't seem to find your way out," Maniac quipped.

I moved to get off my bike, but Pipe stepped in front of Maniac and folded his arms over his chest. "Try The Bar and save your fists from getting bloodied by hitting Maniac."

"Give me a name for the bar and I'll consider not pummeling Maniac's face."

Pipe chuckled. "I did."

"It's called The Bar?"

"Never said Kales Corners was known for its originality." Pipe stepped back into Maniac, bumping him toward to the clubhouse. "I'll keep an eye on everything while you handle your shit."

"Try not to make a pile of shit I have to deal with when I'm back." I cranked up the bike, still itching to knock Maniac out. "I'll keep track of Boink, though." There wasn't any reason to add more people into The Ultra than needed. They all knew what was going on, but I still didn't want anyone else to get involved unless they absolutely needed to be.

Pipe nodded. "Got it."

I drove away from the clubhouse with a little less weight on my shoulders knowing I didn't have to worry about anything in Weston. Everyone was up to speed about what was going on, and if need be, they could step in to help when it came time.

Now, they also knew what I was doing. I knew within the hour, everyone in the club was going to know I was in Kales Corners with Alice. Give it another hour after that, and all the chicks would know too.

Though, they weren't going to know much because I wasn't even sure what I was doing.

*

CHAPTER 8

ALICE

"I don't mean to alarm you, Bos, but I think we might be getting arrested."

Bos looked up from the pool table. "What in the hell are you talking about, woman?"

I watched Mark Allen walk through the front door of The Bar with Kales Corners' finest behind him. "Well, I may or may not have made a pit stop outside when I went to bathroom."

"And what the hell did you do on this pit stop?" he demanded.

I grimaced when Mark pointed at me. "I wanted to test a theory."

"Woman," Bos thundered. "You better stop talking in circles and tell me just what your crazy ass did."

I leaned across the pool table. "I may or may not have drawn a huge dick on a certain car's windshield."

"With what?"

This is where I might have broken the law, but I blame the margaritas that Reierson was blending up behind the bar. He was making them strong, and when I had too much tequila, I got a little crazy. On top of the crazy I normally was. So, I was uber crazy Alice when I was on margaritas. "Um, a can of spray paint I found."

"Where in the hell do you find a can of spray paint in a bar?" he thundered. "I didn't know I had to follow your every damn move when I agreed to go out with you. If I would have known that, I would have stayed home with Mazie so she could clip my toenails."

I wrinkled my nose and grimaced. "Ew, Bos. Totally TMI."

"I think my TMI toenails don't have nothing on the fact that you're about to get arrested for tagging someone's car."

It wasn't just someone. It was Mark Allen. The same guy I had locked in my trunk before I went on a joy ride in a bumpy ass field making sure I hit every bump and rut. "We."

Bos shook his head. "Ain't no goddamn 'we' in this, woman."

"You're just gonna abandon me? Our motto is 'no woman left behind,' Bos. You can't abandon ship when the seas start getting rough." I closed my eyes and dropped my chin to my chest. "They're behind me, aren't they?"

Bos stood up slowly. "Evening, gentlemen."

"We're going to need a talk with Ms. Dorman."

Damn. No introduction. No hello. All the niceties were forgone when you broke the law.

"What about? We've just been enjoying a few beverages and playing a couple games of pool tonight."

"I think that's something we need to discuss outside."

That voice sounded familiar. "Mike Billy?" I stood up and turned around slowly.

"It's Officer Mackson now."

A grin slowly spread across my lips. "That's not what I called you when we were behind the old mill ma—"

His cheeks turned beet red and even the tips of his ears colored a pretty shade of pink. "That was a long time ago, Alice. A time that we don't need to revisit." He tried to talk with authority, but it was just laughable. The last time I had seen *Officer Mackson,* he had been speeding away from my house embarrassed as hell from the fact he had gotten a little too *excited* when we had been in the backseat of his Caprice. He had a wet crotch, and I had tears streaming down my face because it had been funny as hell.

Now, the tables had turned. Well, I didn't have a wet crotch, but you got the point.

Mike still looked the same, except now, he was wearing a dark blue police uniform that was ill-fitted and looked to be one size too big.

"If we could go outside where it's a bit quieter, that would be good."

I glanced over at the other officer and smiled. I had no idea who he was, but that might have to do with the fact that he looked to be about thirteen. "I haven't finished my margarita." As if that was going to stop them from arresting me.

"Pretty sure you've had enough to drink, Alice."

Oh, Mark Allen. He was never able to keep his fucking mouth shut. "Last I checked, I didn't ask you, Marky." That would have been a much better delivery if I hadn't slurred "ask" and "you" together. *Damn you, tequila.*

"Just head out with them, Alice. Ain't nothing going to happen." Bos walked around the pool table and laid his cue on the felt top. "You didn't do nothing wrong, darlin'."

Pfft, that was a damn lie, but since Bos sounded so convincing, I was going to roll with it.

I did a curtsy and nodded to the door. "Shall we?" I led the way out the door with the two cops, Mark Allen, and Bos following. This was a scene I never thought would happen. I'm sure to everyone at the bar, they weren't surprised to see it, though. I was Crazy Alice, after all.

"Look, the sun went down," I announced when I pushed the door open.

"That's what happens at night," Bos pointed out.

"Such a smart man," I cooed. I sat down on the curb in front of The Bar.

"You should know that it's dark out since you were out here drawing a *dick* on my windshield!" Mark screamed.

He was always so overdramatic.

Officer No-Name put his hand on Mark's chest and pushed him back two steps. "Calm down, Mr. Allen. We'll get to the bottom of this."

Someone really needed to check this guy's ID because I honestly didn't think he was old enough to drive, let alone be upholding the law in Kales Corners. "Can I see some ID?" There I was again, opening my mouth when I knew I should keep it shut.

Bos nudged my ass with his foot. "Shut the hell up, woman."

I twisted around and looked up at him. "Like you aren't thinking that kid wasn't just sucking on his mama's titty before he came here."

Bos' head snapped up at the sound of a loud bike pulling into the parking lot. "Looks like one of your motorcycle guys are coming to save you."

"What?" I slurred. I turned to the parking lot and about peed my pants when I saw Wrecker pull up directly in front of me. Maybe I *was* going to have a wet crotch by the time this was over.

Mike Billy stood in front of me, blocking the view of Wrecker. He pulled a small notebook out of his pocket and flipped it open. "Name."

I blinked slowly. "Huh?"

"What is your name?" he enunciated slowly.

"I had my tongue down your throat ten years ago, Mike Billy. My name hasn't changed since then."

Bos chuckled and sat down on the curb next to me.

I leaned to the right and saw Wrecker had gotten off his bike and was now standing a couple feet behind Mike Billy, listening. "Hey, Beardilocks." I gave him a jaunty wave and what I thought was a sexy smile but I'm pretty sure it bordered on the line of Jokeresque.

"Name, Alice," Mike Billy demanded, snapping me out of my greeting to Wrecker.

"I'm the drunk one, and even I know how ridiculous you just sounded asking me name while you said me name."

"My," Bos whispered. Maybe he was a good wingman after all. He might have to be an honorary member of the Girl Gang.

"This is protocol. Please just answer his question." This was from Officer No-Name.

"Name," Mike Billy repeated.

"Boobs McGee."

Bos huffed next to me, and I was pretty sure Officer No-Name smiled.

"Name."

"Phil McCracken." I leaned to the side and was pretty sure behind that sexy beard, Wrecker was smiling.

"Name," Mike Billy screeched. He stabbed his pen into the notepad and gave a little growl.

"Do you need a Xanax? I don't have any but I know where yo—"

Bos elbowed me in the side and shook his head. "Shut it, woman."

Probably telling the cop where he could get some drugs wasn't the best idea. If only my brain would have figured that out before I opened my mouth. "The

Walgreens over in Marlton has them. But only if you have a subscription."

"Prescription." Thank God for Bos.

"Prescription. That's totally what I meant."

"Can I ask what's going on here?" Wrecker stepped next to Mike Billy. He towered over him, and the sheer bulkiness of him completely dwarfed Mike Billy.

Mike Billy looked over and had to tilt his head back to look Wrecker in the face and not his chest. "Not sure what it has to do with you, sir." Mike Billy sounded like he went through puberty in that one sentence.

"Everything has to do with Beardilocks." I hiccuped and leaned against Bos. The tequila was running rampant through me now, and my filter was *gone*. "He's the president of the world." See, no filter. I closed my eyes and willed myself to shut up.

"She drew an erect penis on my car!"

A loopy smile spread across my lips. "I forgot you were here, Mark Allen. Thank God, you used your womanly voice to pipe up."

Bos' body shook with laughter under my head. "I'd correct you by saying manly, but you were right on with womanly."

"And, for the record, would we be having this little…whatever this is, if I had drawn a flaccid cock on your car?" He should be thankful it was a hard cock and not a soft Jello-y one.

"What car?" Wrecker asked.

Mark pointed to his car. His piece of shit car, by the way.

Wrecker walked over to it and swiped his finger through the shaft. "It's still wet," he announced.

"That's what she said." Please let that have been said inside my head.

Bos bent over wheezing with laughter, and even Mike Billy let a smile slip.

Wrecker walked over to his bike, grabbed a white cloth, and stalked back to the car. He wiped the windshield and then held up the rag. "It's gone. Nothing happened." He tossed the rag at Mark, then stood in front of me and reached out his hand.

"I think I'm being arrested."

"You can't be arrested when there isn't any evidence." He grabbed my hand and pulled me off the curb.

"The evidence is right here," Mark screeched, holding up the rag which now looked like a shirt.

Bos pointed his finger at Mark. "Arrest him, officers. He's holding the evidence."

Wrecker hauled me over to his bike. He grabbed a helmet from his bag and set it on my head. "Snap that on, babe."

"We were in the middle of questioning her," Mike Billy said. He reached for my arm, but Wrecker stood in front of me.

"I'm not sure why you are pinning this on her. Did she confess to doing it?" Wrecker demanded.

"Well, no," Mike Billy sputtered. "But we have reason to believe that Alice would have done it."

Wrecker turned to look at me. "You do it?"

I shook my head. "I can barely walk a straight line, let alone draw a stellar penis."

"Stellar?" Bos called.

I leaned around Wrecker to look at Bos. "I totally meant that. Did you see how awesome that dick looked?"

Bos nodded. "Guess it was a pretty good dick." His eyes bugged out, and he stood up. "I need to get the hell out of here. Saying shit I never thought I would," he muttered. "You taking her home?" he asked Wrecker.

Wrecker nodded. "I got her."

"Later, Crazy." Bos gave me a two-finger salute and headed in the direction of his house on foot.

"Never thought I would like that ol' man, but here I am, liking his old ass."

"Heard that," he yelled from the sidewalk.

"What are we going to do about my car?"

Ugh, back to Mark Allen. Stuffing him in my trunk was one of the best decisions I had ever made. Too bad it seemed like I was forever going to have to deal with him being a bitch about everything.

"Your car is fine," Wrecker growled.

I had to appreciate the fact Wrecker was here to save the day. Pretty sure I would have wound up in the back of a police car if it hadn't been for him. I ducked back behind Wrecker and tried to fasten my helmet. This was going to take all of my concentration.

"I hate to admit it, but he's right. We didn't know she had done it in the first place, and now that everything has been cleaned up, there isn't anything else to do." Mike Billy flipped his tiny notebook shut and stuck it in his chest pocket.

"Knew I always liked you, Mike Billy," I muttered. I had both ends of the buckle in my hand and stuck my tongue out to up my concentration on getting them together.

"Why do you call him that?" Officer No-Name asked.

"'Cause it's his name." I tried to join the two ends together and missed stunningly. "Take two," I whispered.

"It is not my name," Mike Billy insisted.

I took a deep breath and peeked around Wrecker at him. "You were okay with me calling you that while you ca—"

"Stop!" he shouted. "My name is Michael William. Not Mike Billy."

Wrecker laughed. At least, I'm pretty sure that was what the noise was I heard come from him. Also, his mammoth shoulders gave a little shake. He had to have laughed. Score one for drunk Alice.

"Now everyone be quiet. I'm hunting bunny wabbits." I tried to get the two ends together but was yet again fouled by the damn thing.

"Did she just say she was hunting bunny wabbits?" Office No-Name asked.

"With Alice, you get used to her weird real quick," Mike Billy quipped.

"That's Boobs McGee to you, Mike Billy." I held the ends of the strap up close to my nose. "Time for you two bastards to meet and get it on."

Wrecker turned around, grabbed the ends from me, and snapped them together. "I'd like to get home tonight, babe." He looked down at me with a smile peeking out from his beard.

Wow. Beardilocks wasn't pissed off at me. From the glint in his eye, he seemed rather happy. "You have the whitest teeth I have ever seen." Yeah, I was a real charmer.

"Thanks, babe. Now get on the bike and try not to fall off."

Seemed like a simple enough task. I patted him on the shoulder. "I so got this. Is it okay if I touch your handlebar?" It was an innocent question, but it also sounded like a dirty innuendo that I would have said. "I mean your actual handlebar." My eyes dropped to his crotch. "Not *that* handlebar."

"I got you, babe."

"Not that I wouldn't touch your handlebar if I had permission." My God. I just couldn't stop. "If the Earth could open up right now and swallow me, that would be great," I whispered.

Wrecker leaned close and pressed his lips to my ear. "You always have permission."

Jumping Jehoshaphat. Even in my drunken mind, I knew Wrecker had very blatantly flirted with me. "Uh, good to know." I cringed and spun around to face his bike.

"We'll be heading home tonight, officers. Thanks for taking care of Alice for me 'til I got here. It's good to know Kales Corners has such a thorough and understanding police department that doesn't jump to conclusions without all the facts."

I swung my leg over the bike and plopped my ass down on the padded seat. "This is way better than the back of a police car." Wrecker, Mike Billy, and Officer No-Name all stared at me. "Puhleeze. Like you all really thought I've never had that honor before." I scoffed, scooted to the back of the seat, and patted in front of me. "Come on, Wrecker. I'm ready to feel the wind on my thighs and the vibrations in my hair."

Officer No-Name raised a finger and sputtered to talk.

Wrecker shook his head. "Think you mean that the other way around, babe, unless you plan on riding with your head where your ass is right now." Wrecker climbed on the bike and cranked it up.

I squinted and thought about what I had just said. "You know what I meant," I hollered.

"This is complete bullshit," Mark Allen yelled. He stomped his foot and raised the white shirt that was smeared with green spray paint. "Who is responsible for the dick, if not her?"

Wrecker walked the bike backward out of his parking spot while Mike Billy and Officer No-Name tried to calm down Mark.

Wrecker turned his head to look at me. "Put your arms around me, babe."

Another simple request that I was more than happy to comply with. "Whatever you want, Beardilocks."

Wrecker rocketed out of the parking lot and down the road in the opposite direction of my house.

"Where are we going?" I hollered in his ear as he rolled through a stop sign. He was headed out of town.

"Going for a ride, babe. The air will do ya good." He took a left at the grocery store then floored it.

It wasn't like I could argue with him. His bike was damn loud, and I didn't want to nag him while he drove.

So, I was going for a ride with Wrecker because the air would do me good.

Whatever the hell that meant.

But honestly, even though it didn't make all that much sense to me, I wasn't going to complain.

I was drunk off margaritas and on the back of Wrecker's bike with my body plastered against him.

This was way better than being arrested for painting a stellar dick on Mark Allen's car.

*

CHAPTER 9

WRECKER

I drove for an hour before I felt her body relax against me.

"Wake up, babe." I grabbed her arm, and she startled against my back.

"I'm up."

Bullshit, she was. I shouldn't have driven for so long with her on the back since she was drunk. I didn't need her falling asleep and becoming a speed bump on the road.

Five miles back, I had spotted a sign for a motel. "Stay awake for five more minutes," I called.

She laid her head on my shoulder. "Trying," she mumbled. "The bike is putting me to sleep." I lightly pinched the skin on her arm, and she yelped. "Really?" she yelled.

"Woke ya up, didn't it?"

We drove ten more minutes before we rolled into town and I saw the motel that had been advertised. The parking lot was empty except for two cars.

"What are we doing?" she asked.

I pulled into a parking spot outside the front office and killed the engine. "Getting a room. You're not going to be able to make it home."

She sat back, and the cool night air met my back where she had been plastered against me. "How do you even know where we are?"

I didn't know where we were. I had just driven because I wanted to keep Alice on the bike with me. "It matter where we are? Climb off," I ordered.

"No. This place looks like Norman Bates' cousin's."

I glanced over my shoulder at her. "Where the hell do you come up with this stuff?"

She shrugged. "It just comes out."

"I'm gonna go see if they have any rooms available. You coming?"

She rolled her eyes and scooted off the bike. "You're not leaving me behind to be the first one killed. I've watched scary movies before, and this is how they always start. Not today, Satan. I ain't ready to die."

I got off the bike, grabbed her hand, and drug her behind me. "I've seen scary movies before, too. They're filled with dumb people. You ain't dumb, babe."

She sputtered and wrapped her other hand over my bicep. "That's not a common assumption about me."

"Assuming something only makes an ass out of people."

I pushed open the door and walked in with Alice attached to me.

The guy behind the desk lifted his head from the computer screen in front of him and plastered a huge smile on his face. "Hello, folks. So happy you decided to stop at the Hideaway."

"What do they hide here, bodies?" Alice hissed.

"We need a room for the night."

"You are in luck. We happen to have a few to choose from." He clicked away on his computer. "Would you like something in front or by the pool?"

"They have a pool?" Alice gasped. One minute, she was worried about dead bodies, and now, she was excited they had a pool.

I leaned against the desk and pulled Alice to my side. She didn't let go of my hand, and I wasn't about to shrug her off. "One by the pool."

"Nice choice, nice choice," he muttered. "We just so happened to have renovated the one I just put you in." He grabbed two cards from the pile and ran them through a small machine. "I'll just need a credit or debit card, and you two will be good to go."

I grabbed my wallet and laid a credit card on the desk. "You guys got breakfast?"

"Sure do, sure do." This guy was into repeating himself. A lot. "Every morning from six to eleven."

"Waffles?" Alice piped up.

"Yup, yup. We have got the waffles, little lady." He winked at her. "They happen to be a favorite of mine especially when I put a few chocolate chips in them." He swiped my credit card, printed off a receipt, and wrote down the plate number on the bike.

"Anything else I can get you two folks?" He handed back my card and the two room keys.

"No. We're good. Just point us in the direction we need to go."

"Head around the building and you will be the room right in front of the entrance to the pool. Three-twelve."

I nodded and tugged Alice out the front door.

"Thank you," Alice called before the door shut. "You could have said thank you," she scolded me.

I threw a leg over the bike. "I nodded."

She rolled her eyes and hopped on behind me. "Try words next time, caveman."

I backed the bike a few steps and cranked the wheel. "I think I like Beardilocks better."

*

CHAPTER 10

ALICE

"Is there a coin slot next to the bed?" This was the strangest but most amazing hotel room I had ever been in before. When the guy at the front desk said it was recently renovated, he must have meant back in the eighties.

Wrecker kicked off his boots and reached into his pocket. He held up a quarter and smirked. "Only one way to find out, babe."

Like I was going to miss the chance to try it out. I grabbed the quarter and dove onto the bed. "Here we go." I dropped the quarter in the slot and nothing happened. "What a freakin' bummer."

Wrecker walked over to the end of the bed and gave it a kick.

"Holy shit," I screamed when the bed started shimming and shaking under me. "Ho-o-o-w i-i-i-s-s-s t-his se-e-e-xy?" I chattered. I rolled over onto my back, thinking maybe it would be a good massage.

"You gonna sleep like that?"

I slapped my hand over my mouth as my stomach rolled, and I swallowed down the margaritas that were begging to make a reappearance.

Wrecker grabbed my arm, hauled me off the bed, and I stood shakily. I slapped my hand on his shoulder and closed my eyes.

"You good, babe?" he asked.

I reached up and plastered my hand over his face. "Shh...The room is moving."

"Maybe the vibrating bed wasn't the best idea with a stomach full of booze."

I nodded. "Instant regret," I moaned.

He wrapped his arms around me and pulled me to his chest. "Deep breath, babe."

"I'm going to have to sleep on the floor. The bed of shakes is a no-go for me."

He chuckled and gave me a squeeze. "It'll turn off, babe."

Hmm, the damn thing was still shaking like an earthquake with no signs of stopping. "We should have gotten snacks."

Wrecker buried his head in my hair. "You go from puking to snacks in five seconds flat, babe."

"I'm complicated like that," I quipped. Besides, once he had gotten me off the bed, my stomach had quieted. "Pringles are always a good idea anyway."

"How about we see if we can order a pizza?"

I leaned back, and he raised his head. "I have never heard more sexier words come out of your mouth."

"Breadsticks?"

I fanned my face with my hand. "Sweet nibblets, Wrecker. I don't think I can handle this. Pizza *and* breadsticks. Between the beard and your ability to tune into my snacking needs, I might never let you out of this room."

"You're crazy, babe."

"I know," I sighed. "I hear it all the time." And while it was true, it got pretty damn annoying to hear constantly. "Sometimes, I'd like to hear something new than the usual 'you're so crazy.'" The bed finally stopped shaking, and I kicked off my shoes. Now, I could lie down without wanting to throw up.

He brushed my hair back from my face and tucked it behind my ear. "Hit a sore spot?"

I shrugged. "Not really. Just a bit annoying to hear all the time." I reached up and threaded my fingers through his beard. "You could make up for it by buying me pizza, though."

"Food fixes most things with you, huh?"

"For the most part."

"And what are the things that food doesn't fix?"

I tugged gently on his beard. "Are we really going to go there tonight? I'm drunk and hungry."

"I can fix the hungry part and start drinking water. It's been over an hour since you've had a drink, anyway."

"So that means we are going there, huh?"

He chuckled and shook his head. "We're talking, babe, not going to Africa."

"Well, we're going to need snacks *and* pizza before we talk or go to Africa."

He pulled out his phone and handed it to me. "Order pizza. I'll run to the gas station on the corner and get snacks."

"Wait, I'll go with you to get snacks. You don't know what I like." I held his phone out to him.

He pushed my hand away and walked to the door. "Pringles and every other junk food the place has to offer. Sound about right?"

Well, that was a good place to start. "I like Coke. The soda, not the drug."

He stroked his beard and laughed. "Not a drug run, good to know."

I rolled my eyes and flipped him off. "You're an ass."

"We've gone over this before, babe. You calling me an ass doesn't bother me."

"Who said I'm trying to bother you? I'm just stating a fact." I crossed my arms over my chest and took a step back.

"Your facts are shit, babe. I'm an ass, but I've hardly been that to you."

I think his definition of an ass was way different than mine. "Um, you coming over all the time, telling me what to do, and well, just being you is ass-ish."

"Ass-ish?" he drawled.

"Nothing I say right now can be held against me because I'm drunk-ish."

"That would mean everything you've ever said to me can't be held against you."

I tapped my finger to my chin. "That's not entirely true. I think when I first met you, I hadn't been drinking."

"Babe, you fucking curtsied."

"Not sure what your point is right now."

He took a step closer. "Who the hell curtsies?"

"I thought it was respectful because you are the president."

"Of a motorcycle club, babe, not of the country."

"Tomatoes, toMAtoes," I shrugged. "They're both pretty impressive in my book."

"I think you just gave me a compliment."

I scoffed and shook my head. "I did no such thing. I curtsied before I knew you."

"So, you wouldn't curtsy to me now?"

He took another step closer, and I stepped back. I grabbed onto Wrecker's shoulders before I went ass-over-tea kettle. "Does it really matter?" I stammered.

He wrapped his arms around my waist and splayed his hands across my back. "Need to know if I should keep going down the path I'm on."

"Uh, this path? I can tell you, if you keep walking this way, you'll only end up in bed." I looked over my shoulder. "Yeah, totally a bed there."

He leaned down and brushed his lips across my ear. "That's exactly where I'm headed, babe. Taking you with me, too."

"Too?" I squeaked. He pulled me close, and I turned my head to look at him. "I'm a little intoxicated and confused on what is going on here."

"Nah, babe. You know exactly what is going on here. You just like to bury your head in the sand and ignore all the signs."

"Signs?" I was like a parrot repeating everything he said.

"Why do you think I keep showing up, Alice?"

I gulped. "Uh, cause you're an ass."

"My ass has nothing to do with this."

Now all I could think about was his ass and how I hoped it had something to do with this. "You're awfully close to me."

"Yeah," he whispered.

"Um, why?"

"Because being close to you is the only thing that makes sense when you're around."

I nodded. I didn't get any of this. "Completely at a loss here, Wrecker. I have no idea what to say."

"I think that's part of your problem, babe. You think you always need to have something to say when sometimes, silence says it all."

"Silence and I don't really do well together." I talked to myself when I was all alone. That was proof that silence was not something I did. Ever.

"How about we give it another try"

"Give wha—"

He closed the distance between us and brushed his lips against mine. "Shh." His lips captured mine, and he kissed me.

It was nice.

My God, was it nice.

It was gentle.

Unhurried.

He kissed me like there was nothing else in the world except for me and him. My fingers clenched his shirt between them, and I tried to feel everything at once.

His scratchy yet soft beard brushing against my chin.

The way his hands rested on my hips, holding me in place.

His scent. My God, did this man smell good. I was going to find out what cologne he wore and dump it on my pillow at home.

He broke the kiss and whispered against my lips. "See how silence can be a good thing, babe?"

Now that was some silence that I could get used to having in my life. I involuntarily made a mewling noise in the back of my throat, and his eyes darkened with lust.

He had rendered me speechless. I didn't want to talk; all I wanted to do was kiss him. At least fifty million more times.

My hands moved up, snaking around his neck, and I delved my fingers into his hair in the back. "I might be a fan of that kind of silence."

"Figured you would be up to it," he drawled. He kissed me again. This time, taking instead of just giving. His beard scraped along my chin and my hands itched to bury my fingers in it. I was borderline obsessed with touching his beard. Being this close to it was almost orgasmic.

His lips trailed along my jawline and down my neck. "You taste like fucking watermelon, babe."

Thank you, Bath and Body Works. "Oh yeah?" I gasped. "You somehow smell like freedom and sex."

His lips froze on my skin, and his hands squeezed my hips. "Come again?"

Where the hell was my filter when I needed it? "Uh, I mean you smell nice too. Not like watermelon, but…"

"Freedom and sex?" he laughed.

Ugh. Kill me now. I was forever destined to be making a fool of myself. "Yeah."

"Gonna have to take your word for that one because I'm not sure what that smells like. Just put cologne on each morning."

"What kind?" I asked desperately. Here was my shot to buy stock in whoever made it.

"Rag and Bone."

I had never heard of it before, but I committed the name to memory. "I like it."

"Kind of figured that."

I bit my lip. "Uh, can we get back to silence?"

"Anything for you, babe." His lips claimed mine again. I didn't think I would ever get used to the thrill that coursed through me when his lips touched me. The softness of his lips with the light scratch of his beard was an intoxication sensation I never wanted to lose.

His arms wrapped around me, and he walked me back 'til my calves hit the mattress, and we tumbled onto the bed.

"Look, we made it to your destination," I giggled.

"Sure did, babe." His hands traveled up my sides, tugging my shirt up and over my breasts. A low growl rumbled from his throat. "Damn."

I raised my arms and laid them over my head. "Now you know what I think every time I touch your beard."

His eyes looked up from my breasts. "You have a slight obsession with my beard."

It was a statement rather than a question. "Um, yes." There was really no point in denying it. Maybe with him knowing, he would let me have my way with it.

"You're thinking about it, aren't you?"

"Well, it's right in front of me," I whined. "You're taunting me with it."

A sexy as sin smirk crossed his lips. "I bet you wonder what it feels like against your skin."

Lord have mercy, did I. I bit my lip and nodded. "It's possibly crossed my mind a time or two."

He lowered his head, his lips hovering over the bare flesh of my breast. "Wonder what it would feel like if I kissed you right here." His warm breath washed over my skin, teasing me.

"Please," I whispered. I wasn't above begging.

"You taste like watermelon all over?"

"Why don't you find out for yourself?" He wanted to know what I tasted like, and I needed to know what his kisses would feel like all over my body. We could kill two birds with one stone if he would just lower his lips an inch.

His right hand molded to the curve of my hip while the other pulled down the cup of my bra. "I'd die a happy man right now if God took me," he rasped.

"Let's hope he doesn't take you before you kiss me again."

He looked up, and his eyes connected with mine. "I take you in my mouth, babe, I'm not going to be able to stop."

It was a warning. One I should have heeded. Wrecker wasn't the type of man I usually wound up with. I had run into two of the guys who had spent time with me, and each of them now made my skin crawl from the fact I had let them touch me.

If this was only destined to happen once with Wrecker, I knew if I ever ran into him after, he would set my skin on fire, not make it crawl.

Wrecker was everything that was probably going to be bad for me, but I didn't care. He was rough, gruff, and demanding. He barely laughed and was always bossing me around. He should piss me off.

He didn't, though.

I wanted him.

I wanted him more than anything I had ever wanted in my life.

"I'm waiting," I whispered. I wasn't going to turn down my chance to share my bed with this man. I would be a fool to say no.

He didn't wait.

He didn't hesitate.

He had given me a chance to run, but I was still in this thing. I'd always had an attraction to Wrecker, and the more time I spent with him, the more I realized what a good guy he was. A little rough around the edges, but still a good guy.

Wet kisses were pressed against my breasts, his mouth traveling back and forth between the two as though he didn't want one to have more attention than the other. "Watermelon," he mumbled.

"Heaven," I replied. His mouth was better than anything I had ever imagined. This man should be registered as a lethal weapon from the things he made me feel. Just the brush of his mouth on me was almost more than I could take. Almost. "Don't stop doing that. Ever."

I felt his body rumble and knew he was laughing at me again. Oh well. He could laugh all he wanted when his lips were on me.

"Sit up." He grabbed my hands and pulled me up while he sat back in-between my legs. His hands were pulling my shirt over my head and circling around me to unclasp my bra before I could even blink.

"Holy cannolis." He pulled his shirt over his head, and all logical thought fled. I knew from his arms that he was tattooed, but I didn't know exactly what was hiding under his shirt.

My eyes feasted on loads of ink and bulging muscles. He had muscles in places I didn't even know had muscles. I knew the man was built like a brick shit house, but just *damn*. "I bet you could lift me over your head." I needed to start keeping tally of all the dumb things I said in front of him. Though, if I did, I would probably die of embarrassment at the extremely high number.

He ignored me. That worked well for my ego.

His arms reached for me, and I gladly fell into them. I wrapped my arms around his neck, my body pressed against him, and I arched my back. He trailed kisses across my collarbone, his beard tickling my skin along the way. His hands palmed my ass, and he lifted me onto lap, my tits right in his face. "Whoa."

He didn't say anything. He couldn't. His mouth was full of my breast.

"Wrecker," I moaned. I had never been one to go off from just a little bit of kissing, but with Wrecker, everything I thought I knew about myself went out the window because I was seconds away from pulling a Mike Billy and coming with my pants still on.

He toppled us over on the bed. His mouth left my breast and claimed my mouth. He grabbed my hands and held them over my head while he kissed me. The weight of his body on top of me felt like a blanket that I never wanted to get out from under. "Keep your arms there," he ordered.

I wasn't going to argue because he was more than in charge of what was going on, and I was totally fine with that.

He sat back on his heels, popped open the buttons on my jeans, and worked them down my legs. "You got a thing for cows, babe?"

"Huh?" That was an odd thing to ask when you were taking someone's pants off.

"Your pajamas, and now your underwear, babe."

I looked down my body and remembered I had slid on my cow print boy shorts this morning. "I tend to gravitate toward it." At least, when it came to pajamas and underwear. Although, I did have a killer skirt hanging in my closet dying to be worn.

He hooked his thumbs in the waistband and slowly tugged them down my legs. "Well, they're going to gravitate onto the floor right now, babe."

"More than okay with that," I sighed. "I'd be okay if your pants and underwear joined them too." No sense in my underwear getting lonely down there.

"In due time," he muttered. "Scoot your head up to the pillow."

I awkwardly slid myself up the bed on my elbows 'til my head hit the pillow. "You're really bossy." I thought it was best to point that out to him while I did exactly what he told me. It somehow made it feel like I was protesting a little bit even though I wasn't.

He rested his hands on my thighs and pushed my legs apart. "Who would have known all it would take for you to listen to me was to get you naked."

"Guess I only listen to you when I don't have clothes on."

He chuckled and laid down on his stomach between my legs. His face was directly in front of my pussy, and I tried to focus on the words coming out of his mouth. "I'll have to remember that, babe."

"Huh?" God, I was a mess. "What are we remembering?"

He chuckled and splayed his hand over my pussy. "Damn, you're cute."

"Um, thank you?" What were you supposed to say when someone calls you cute but had a hand over your pussy? Thank you seemed like a safe bet.

A tremor rocked through my body when he leaned forward and pressed kisses where his hand had been. "One last place to find out what you taste like."

Oh, heavens above. I was going to combust on the spot. "Mmkay." Wasn't going to argue with him wanting to find out. It was also the last place I craved to know what his mouth would feel like.

His fingers parted the lips of my pussy, and the cool air sent a chill through me in anticipation. "Dripping," he growled. That would be his damn fault. Pretty sure it was a swampy mess of need and desire down there.

His tongue flicked my clit, and I dug my heels into the mattress. "Sweet burritos. Give a girl a little bit of warning before you go straight for the buzzer," I gasped.

He ignored me once again. He seemed to be good at that. He was also good with his tongue. So damn good.

"Shush, babe," he ordered.

"Silence," I whispered.

He sucked my clit into his mouth as my reward for shutting my mouth. It wasn't going to take much to make me go off like a rocket.

He lifted his head from my pussy and pressed a kiss to my inner thigh. "Sweet as fuck." His beard tickled the inside of my leg, and I bucked my hips. This was all too much. I didn't know what to feel first. His words went straight to my head while my body freaked the hell out whenever he touched me.

His mouth returned to my spread pussy, honing in on my clit, while one of his fingers gently probed my hole. His tongue altered from licking and flicking while he thrust inside me.

Jesus, Mary, and Joseph, I was in Heaven. Nothing in life would ever beat this moment.

I dropped my hands and delved them into his hair. I would have buried them in his beard but his face was otherwise occupied at the moment. His name escaped my lips when I slammed my eyes shut and felt my orgasm wash over me. I dug my heels into the bed and lifted my ass to press my pussy up to his mouth.

"Ah, stop, stop," I groaned. This was too much. My body was going to start gearing up to come again if he kept it up.

He pressed sweet, soft kisses along the insides of my thighs while my body came down from the amazing high he had sent me on. "Don't move," he whispered.

My ass wasn't going anywhere because my legs were Jell-O, and there was no way in hell I was going to be able to walk.

I opened my eyes, watched him drop his pants to the floor, and was pleasantly surprised by the ink on his legs and the fact that he didn't wear underwear. His dick bobbed heavily between his legs, and I popped my elbows under me to get a better view.

"Wowzas."

He chuckled and ran his fingers through his beard. "Never have a fucking clue what's gonna come out of that mouth of yours."

I shrugged. "It's normally a crapshoot of what I'm going to say. Half the time, I don't even know what I'm going to say until it's out of my mouth."

He dropped a knee onto the bed and twirled his finger in the air. "Flip over on your stomach."

I did what he asked because I was naked, and his dick was "wowza" amazing.

"On your hands and knees."

A chill ran through my body at his command. He was so going to fuck me doggie style. "Yippee," I whispered as I got my knees under me.

"Wowza and yippee," he muttered. "Gonna have to get you some better words for when I'm about to fuck you, babe." I dropped my head to the pillow and moaned. The bed shifted as he moved behind me and ran a hand over the curve of my ass. "I know your pussy is dripping wet for me. I wonder if I can make you come again for me."

Just from his words alone, I could come again. "May the odds ever be in your favor," I murmured.

He lightly smacked my ass and growled. "Quiet."

"You got it, Beardilocks," I whispered.

His laid his hand on the small of my back while the other moved down my ass and found my clit again. "God damn, Alice. You're fucking dripping."

Hey, there ain't no shame in my game. The man drove me insane with need, and my body was letting him know I was ready to get it on.

"Watch me," he growled. "Look at me."

I got my arms underneath me and looked over my shoulder at him. His hand was wrapped around his dick poised at the entrance to my pussy. I licked my lips silently and made note I wanted to find out what he tasted like. "Can I say something?" I asked. I know, I know. I couldn't keep my mouth shut. It was something I was going to have to work on. Though I'm sure Wrecker was going to work on it too by the look he gave me.

"About to bury my dick inside you, babe, and you got something to say other than screaming my name?"

I clicked my tongue and slightly shook my head back and forth, debating if I wanted to say anything. "I plan on screaming your name, don't worry about that. I just wanted to say, I'm like uber excited for this." Uber. Add that to the list of words not to say during sex.

Wrecker chuckled and shook his head. "Can I fuck you now, or do you have more cute shit to say?"

I probably did have some more weirdness I could spew but I thankfully thought it through and shook my head.

"Head down, ass up," he growled.

He was going to need a fire extinguisher to put out the fire if he kept talking like that. Who would have thought Wrecker's crude mouth would be a *huge* turn-on for me? Though Wrecker as a whole got my engine running more than anyone else.

I dropped my face back to the pillow and arched my back to position my ass right into his hand that was still stroking his dick.

"Eager," he mumbled.

Eager didn't even begin to describe it. I was fucking ready.

He slowly pushed inside me, his "wowza" dick stretching and filling me.

This was good.

Fucking good.

He slowly thrust in and out, his hands holding my hips as his fingertips dug into my skin. "Feel it, babe."

Oh, I felt it. Lord have mercy, did I feel it.

Everything Wrecker did, he did with purpose. And his purpose right now was to make me come for a second time. The only difference this time was, I was going to come all over his dick.

I liked the feel of us together. He thrusted in, I reared back, slamming into him, and when he pulled out, I rocked forward. We worked in tandem, each searching for the thrust to knock us both over the edge.

Wrecker went first, but as soon as he growled out my name, I was following right behind him with my pussy wringing his cock dry. His hands held me tightly, his dick buried in me root to tip, while I tried not to fall over.

He slapped my ass, then leaned over to press a kiss to my shoulder. "Now that is how you fuck, babe."

I couldn't argue with that statement. Being with Wrecker had been off the damn charts. There wasn't anything to complain about from his magical mouth to his wowza dick. He had rocked my world, and I was worried it was never going to be the same after that.

He fell to the side, and I collapsed into the bed like a limp noodle. "Thank you," I wheezed. What could I say? I was polite.

He draped his arm across me and pulled me to his side. "You're welcome, babe, but I'm pretty sure I should be the one saying thank you." He worked the covers from under us and pulled them over us.

"I need to go clean up."

He tossed back the blanket. "Hurry back."

I giggled and pressed a kiss to his shoulder. "I think I should be the one saying that to you since you still need to make a run for Pringles and junk food while I clean up and order pizza."

He looked down at me. "I just fucked the hell out of you, and now you want pizza?"

"A girl has needs," I explained.

"I thought I just took care of all of those needs but I can see I didn't."

I slid out of bed and looked down at him. "I was hungry before, now I'm starving. It's really your fault."

He threw back the covers. "And what am I going to get out of running to the gas station for you?"

My eyes were glued to his dick that was still at half-mast, and I licked my lips. "I was thinking there might be a part of you I want to find out what it tastes like."

He jumped out of bed and grabbed his jeans off the floor. "Get cleaned up, order the damn pizza, and I'll be back in twenty minutes." He yanked his shirt over his head and sat down on the bed to put his boots on. "Nineteen minutes, babe. Get your ass moving."

I skipped into the bathroom and partially shut the door behind me. I took care of business, and Wrecker hollered that he was leaving. I heard the door shut and looked into the mirror.

My hair was an absolute mess and my body was flushed a pleasant shade of pink. I ran my fingers through my hair, hoping to tame the mane. "We've learned one thing from this," I mumbled. I leaned forward and smiled. "Promises of blow jobs motivates Wrecker."

Now, I was going to get pizza, snacks, and a taste of Wrecker for dessert.

That was what I called a good ending to the night.

*

CHAPTER 11

WRECKER

"This is the breakfast of champions."

Alice was laid out on the bed with her head on my stomach while she munched on cold pizza.

"Nah, pretty sure me eating your pussy this morning was the breakfast of champions."

She choked on the bite she had just swallowed and hammered on her chest. "You can't say stuff like that without warning," she wheezed.

"Now you know what it's like for me when you blurt out whatever comes to mind."

She rolled her eyes and sat up to grab her soda from the nightstand. "When I do it, it's adorable."

"And what about when I do it?"

She looked over her shoulder at me. "It's just...I don't know."

I wrapped my arms around her waist and pulled her to my side. "Nice explanation," I chuckled.

She shrugged. "I thought it was. Save the randomness for me." She winked and pressed a kiss to my lips. "What are you going to do with me today, Mr. President?"

"Why don't we go to Weston? We're only about forty minutes away."

She stiffed in my arms. "Uh, really?"

"Yeah."

She twisted and laid her arms on my shoulders. "Can we drop me at home first?"

I shook my head. "Babe. We're going to Weston cause we're forty minutes away. I take you back home, I ain't going to Weston."

"Perfect," she chirped. "We can just go home."

I wrapped my arms around her, grabbed her lush ass, and pulled her on top of me. "We need to finish our talk from last night because what we were going to talk about last night has to do with the reason why you don't want to go to Weston."

She wrinkled her nose. "That's a hard pass for me." She poked a finger into my chest. "You know what we should do? Go find mimosas. That sounds *way* better than talking."

"Not happening, babe. We talk and then maybe I'll find you a drink." We weren't going to find any mimosas in this town, but I wasn't about to let her know that.

"You get three questions, Mr. President, and that's it."

"And you have to answer them." I knew if I didn't say that, she was going to somehow get out of answering them.

She rolled her eyes. "I hate you." She sat back and looked down at me. "Ask away."

"Why don't you want to go to Weston with me? You know Nikki wants to see you, and you haven't even seen Cole yet." I wasn't going to beat around the bush with her about this. She had people who cared about her and wanted to see her. She wasn't going to blow them off.

"I've been busy. Next question."

"We ain't done with that one, babe. What the hell have you been busy with?"

"I don't want to do this." She shifted to move off me, but I splayed my hands around her waist.

"Stay."

"I don't want to do this, Wrecker. Please let me go," she said quietly.

I never force anyone to do something they didn't want to do, but I knew the only way Alice was going to get past whatever the hell was going on inside her head was to talk about it. "Not until you tell me why, Alice."

I felt the change in her. She went from happy, to sad, and now pissed the hell off. She laid her hands on my chest and leaned down on them. "Why what, Wrecker? Why don't I want to see my friends? Because I have to tell them where I've been. Why I haven't been around. Why don't I want to tell them where I've been?" She took a deep breath. "Because then I have to talk about my mother. My mother who died exactly eleven days ago. My mother who was my absolute world and is now gone." She gritted her teeth and fought the tears that were clogging her throat. "I had one person left in this world who cared about me, and now they are gone. I don't want to go to Weston because then, I have to think about her, and when I think about her, all I want to do is cry." She dissolved into a mess of tears and sniffling. I pulled her down to my chest and wrapped my arms around her.

There wasn't anything I could say to make her feel better. She had to go through it. She had to feel the loss. There wasn't rhyme or reason to how she should feel or what she should do. Some people surrounded themselves with people when they felt a loss. Others, like Alice, didn't want to be with anyone. They felt their world had been tipped on its axis and sank into that.

She was wrong saying the only person who had cared about her was gone. She had Nikki, Karmen, Cora, and Wren back in Weston who were her friends. All the guys in the club thought she was crazy, but they didn't want anything to happen to her.

I cared about her. I hadn't been in her life for long, but I cared about her more than she knew. After spending the last week or so with her, I got to know her for more than her crazy ass and one-liners. "Just breathe, babe."

Hiccups rocked her body, and she wiped her face with the back of her hand. "This is wh-why I don't want to talk about this, Wrecker. I'm a hot m-m-mess."

"You gotta get it out."

She laid her head back down and shook it back and forth. "I don't want it out. I don't want anyone to know. It's mine, Wrecker, and you can't make me talk about it."

I would give her more time, but she wasn't going to keep that grief bottled up for forever. "You don't have to tell anyone, babe, but you can talk to me about it whenever you want. I'll listen." I didn't want her to think I would preach at her or tell her to get over it if she talked about it. A loss like the one she had wasn't one she would ever get over.

"You do a lot of listening to me, don't you?" she whispered.

"I do." I brushed my hand down her back. "But I think we should go to Weston today."

Her body tightened, and she shook her head. "No, Wrecker. I just told you all the reasons why I don't want to. I can't talk about my mom today. I can't be a blubbering mess all day."

"You don't need to tell them today, babe."

"They're gonna ask where I've been. Why I haven't called or texted."

"You can tell them I've been keeping you too busy to do anything but work and stay in bed."

She lifted her head and looked at me in disbelief. "You're crazy. You know that's just going to open up a whole other can of worms. All they're gonna do is ask who, what, when, where, and how. Mostly the how. I wasn't on your radar before this."

No one had been on my radar before her. I had chicks I would sleep with occasionally, but there wasn't anyone I went back to time and again. I had noticed Alice before, but I knew she was the kind of light someone like me didn't get to stand in. "Just tell 'em it happened and the details aren't any of their business."

"That only works for you, Wrecker. All you do is scowl at someone and they wouldn't ask you where the fire extinguisher was if they were on fire."

That was a good skill to have. Sometimes, you didn't have time to tell people to fuck off. A look was all you had to get the point across sometimes. "You need me to give that look to your girls, just let me know."

A giggle bubbled from her lips. "I think if I did that, they'd never talk to me again."

"Your choice, babe."

She sighed and laid her head back down on my chest. "You're gonna make me go even though I don't want to, aren't you?" she mumbled.

"I am."

*

CHAPTER 12

ALICE

I needed a drink. A big one.

We had pulled up to the clubhouse, and my heart was beating a mile a minute. "Oh darn, doesn't look like anyone is here."

Wrecker shook his head. "Never mind the seven bikes and four cars," he mumbled. "Hop off."

Argh. Damn him for driving us here. I slid off the bike and waited off to the side as he stood up. I unhooked the helmet and held it out to him. "Is there a reason why I have to wear a helmet and you don't have to?"

He grabbed it and hung it on the handlebars. "Precious cargo, babe."

I tried to act like his words didn't melt the ice I had formed around my heart on the drive over here. I was mad he had decided we were going to come here even when I had told him I didn't want to. I had even given him some pretty darn good excuses too. I hadn't even fed him a line of bullshit either. "Precious cargo you delivered to a place it doesn't want to be."

He grabbed my hand and tugged me toward the front door. "You'll thank me later."

"Wait." I tugged on his hand, and he surprisingly stopped. "I really don't have to tell them. Anything?"

"They ask where you been, tell 'em you've been with me. They got any more questions, send 'em my way."

This is where the man confused the hell out of me. He was making me do something I didn't want to, but he was making it bearable. More than bearable. He was going to take all the heat off me. "I don't want to lie."

He reached up and cupped my cheek with his hand. "You haven't been with me the past week?"

It had been more than a week. "Well, for some of it, I have been."

"You think they are going to ask for a detailed timeline of what you have been doing, babe?"

"Well, no." That would be ridiculous of they did. "But I know they are going to want to know more than just you and I have been hanging out."

His thumb brushed against my cheek. "Just tell them whatever you feel like. They'll accept anything you have to say as long as you don't keep shutting them out."

"You make this so easy."

"Stick with me, and I'll take care of you, babe." His lips brushed against mine, and I wished for a few moments of silence between Wrecker and me.

"Can't we just sneak into your room? Kind of interested in what it looks like." I wiggled my eyebrows. "Especially your bed."

"Play nice with your friends, and maybe I'll give you a tour."

I wrinkled my nose. "You're always doing that to me. Giving me something but only if I do something else."

"And yet you keep agreeing with everything," he whispered against my lips. "Let's go." He turned around, but I didn't budge 'til my arm was outstretched and I had no choice but to follow him.

I fell in step next to him and sighed. "I'm only doing this because once we get in your room, I'm going to have my way with your beard."

"I'm afraid to ask what all that entails," he murmured.

He pulled open the door, and I ducked inside. "I'm also getting a shirt that says 'I did it all for the beard.'" I looked over my shoulder and winked.

"You're only wearing that shirt when you're with me. Lord knows all the weirdos you'll attract with that plastered over your chest."

I batted my eyelashes. "It sounds like you care, Wrecker."

He wrapped his arm around my waist and pulled me close. It didn't matter where we were or who was around us. When Wrecker put his hands on me, everything disappeared. "I care more than you know, babe." His hand slid up my arm and up my neck. His fingers threaded through my hair and tugged my head back.

Whoa.

He brushed his lips against mine but I wanted more than a brief kiss. I raised up on my tiptoes and followed his retreating lips. "More." Yes, I wanted more.

"Holy fuck."

Shit.

Everything came flooding back. Where we were. Who was here.

Double shit.

"Can't you see I'm fucking busy?" Wrecker growled. He rested his head against mine and closed his eyes. "Maybe we should do that tour of my room first."

Now we were talking. I was so down with that plan.

"Oh. My. God."

And just like that, we were both completely jerked out of the moment. Of course, Pipe and Nikki would be the ones to see Wrecker and me together.

"Pinch me, Pipe," Nikki whispered loudly.

A grin spread across my lips, and Wrecker raised his head. "Can't you both see I got something cooking right now?"

I stood on my tip toes and glimpsed Nikki with her jaw dropped and Pipe standing next to her. Might as well get the fifty questions over with. "Hey," I waved.

"Alice!" Nikki shouted.

"Holy hell," Wrecker muttered. He took a step back right before Nikki ran straight into me and wrapped me up in a hug.

I could have sworn Wrecker mumbled something along the lines of "I told you so," but Nikki was talking a mile a minute and it was hard to keep up, let alone listen to Wrecker's mumbling.

"What are you doing here? How did you get here? Did you come with Wrecker? Was he just kissing you? How is that with a beard? I need to call Karmen to tell her to get here with Cole. How's Bos? Why haven't you called me? How did Wrecker get you?"

My head swam at all the rapid-fire questions. "I can't even answer one of those questions, Nikki, cause I can't even remember one of them."

She released me from her tight hug and took a step back. "What are you doing here?"

"Uh, Wrecker and I were kind of in the neighborhood and decided we should stop." That was kind of the truth. Wrecker had been the one to decide we come, and I was just forced to go along with it.

"That also answered my question of did you come with Wrecker. Was he really just kissing you?"

I looked over my shoulder to see Wrecker had walked over to Pipe and they were deep in conversation. "Uh, yeah, he was kissing me."

Nikki clapped her hands together and squealed. "That is awesome!" She leaned close. "What's it like to kiss him with all of that beard going on?"

Awesome was the word that came to mind. "It's good."

She tilted her head to the side. "Just good?"

"Really good?" I laughed.

She pulled her phone out and typed out a quick message. "I'm sure Karmen will be here as soon as she sees my message." She shoved her phone back in her pocket and continued her questioning. "How's Bos?"

"Uh, good. We went out last night. Almost got arrested."

Nikki's jaw dropped. "You got Bos to go out with you? How the hell did you manage to swing that one?"

"I made him."

She threw her head back and laughed. "Sounds about the only way you can get Bos to do anything."

That was the truth.

"Why haven't you called me lately?"

This was the question I didn't want to answer. I didn't want to tell her, but I knew that as soon as I opened my mouth, everything was just going to rush out.

"I've kept her a little occupied," Wrecker called.

Nikki wiggled her eyebrows. "Now that sounds like a good reason not call or text your best friend."

Wrecker was totally getting a blow job when he showed me his room.

"But how did that happen?" Nikki asked.

"Jesus Christ, Nikki. What the hell kind of question is that?" Pipe asked.

"A valid one," she countered.

"Yeah, well, sounded like you couldn't believe that Wrecker would be interested in Alice."

It had, but I knew what she meant. "Someone has to put up with my crazy, right? At least, for a bit."

Nikki tilted her head to the side.

"You call Karmen?" Pipe asked.

Nikki was looking at me weird. She was thinking about something, and I didn't want to know what it was. "Uh, yeah. I texted her," she replied absently. "Are you sure you're okay?"

Ack! Abort, abort. "Never better." I plastered a huge smile on my face and took a step toward Wrecker. I was going to have to keep the damn man plastered to my side if I wanted to make it through the rest of the day.

"You seem different."

"She's probably tired. I kept her up most of the night."

Nikki's jaw dropped again. "My sweet Jesus."

She really did seem shocked by the fact Wrecker and I were bumpin' uglies. I mean, it had only happened twice, and it was still pretty new, but I didn't think it was all together that shocking.

"So, what are you guys up to? Come to check in on us? It hasn't even been a full damn day since you left," Pipe asked.

Wrecker nodded to the bar. "You want a drink, babe?"

The man was a mind-reader. A drink sounded fucking fantastic. "I'm a little parched."

Nikki laughed. "I was just about to run to the store to get champagne for mimosas. Pipe was giving me shit saying I couldn't bring something that fancy into the clubhouse."

I had been craving a mimosa, but I would have to ride along with Nikki alone. There wasn't a way for Wrecker to come with me without looking like a complete nutbag. Nikki was my friend. We used to hang out all the time when she lived in Kales Corners, and even when she had moved back to Weston to live with Pipe, we stayed in touch. Now I was a fucking weirdo who freaked out about hanging out with her alone.

Wrecker moved toward us and grabbed my hand. "Have Freak run and get it. No reason you two need to get it when we have a perfectly good prospect to run and get shit." He squeezed my hand, and I couldn't ignore the peaceful calm that came over me from his simple touch.

"Well, I'll be damned. The beard and crazy one hooked up." Cora stood by the end of the bar with her hands on her hips. "Tell me I'm not the only who is completely and utterly blown away by this."

"You still here?" Wrecker asked.

She flipped him off. "I'm here 'cause you guys can't seem to get shit figured out."

"You have your brother to thank for all of that, Cora. I'm the one trying to get it straightened out without anyone getting a bullet between the eyes." Wrecked parked me onto a stool, and now, I was the one with my jaw dropped.

"Uh, bullet between the eyes?" I croaked.

Cora spread her arms out. "Welcome to the Fallen Lords, Alice," she laughed. "Though you really don't have anything to worry about when it comes to bullets. Your beard, on the other hand, isn't so lucky." I looked at Wrecker, who was glaring at Cora.

"You got anything better to be doing right now other than scaring my girl?" His voice was flat, with a menacing tone. He wasn't happy. I had hung out with Cora many times, and I knew she didn't know how to keep her mouth shut even when it was in her best interest to do so.

Cora sat down next to me and draped her arm over my shoulders. "Don't look so pale, Alice. Wrecker is good at dodging bullets."

Wrecker shook his head. "Maybe coming here wasn't the best idea," he mumbled.

"Is anyone going to find Freak to have him go get me champagne?" Nikki was still standing by the door with her hands on her hips. "I need to know if I have to go or if he is."

"Freak!" Pipe yelled.

"Because we don't have phones where you can message or call him." Wrecker shook his head and moved to the other side of the bar. He picked up a container of orange juice and shook it. "Tell him to get orange juice, too."

"Oh, my bad. That was totally me last night. I was drinking screwdrivers while I watched some murder mystery show." Cora reached over the bar and grabbed a glass. "They were going down like water while I tried to figure out who would kill the kindergarten teacher."

"Who did it?" I asked,

"Not a fucking clue 'cause I passed out from too many screwdrivers." She cackled and held her empty glass out to Wrecker. "You playing bartender?"

"Not for your ass." He grabbed two glasses, dropped some ice cubes in them, and filled them with water.

"Uh, I think you're forgetting something."

He looked up at me.

"Booze," I whispered.

He set the glass in front of me and shook his head. "Drink that."

Uh, what?

"Is he like this in bed?" Cora asked.

I turned my head to look at her. "Makes me drink water?"

She scoffed and shook her head. "No, dumb-dumb. I mean, is he this bossy."

Oh. That was a definite hell yeah.

"You need to rehydrate from last night before you start drinking again," he cut in before I could reply.

I lifted the glass to my lips. "The answer is yes, Cora. Though it's much sexier when he doesn't have any pants on."

"Drink," he growled.

"Someone yell for me?"

I looked around Cora and saw a guy peeking his head into the common room. He looked like your normal, average guy but he had a cut on like Wrecker.

"Champagne and orange juice," Wrecker called. "Take longer than fifteen minutes and you have to wash my bike."

Cora laughed, and Nikki came to sit next to me. "It's really amazing that you guys manage to get prospects to stay. The liquor store is five minutes away, and I doubt he'll be able to get orange juice there."

I drank half of my water and set it down. "He can. Most liquor stores have common mixers stocked. At least in Kales Corners they do, and Weston is more than twice the size. Though, I have to agree that your way of being an ass doesn't seem to be a good motivator for 'ol Freak."

"You see him get upset about it, babe?" Wrecker drawled.

"Well, no." But it still wasn't nice to tell him to do something and give him a ridiculous deadline that he wasn't going to make.

He rested he forearms on the bar and leaned toward me. "That's why you call me Mr. President, babe." He winked and nudged my glass toward me. "Finish that and I'll see what I can mix up for you 'til the champagne and OJ gets here."

I glared at him but downed the rest of my water. He so wasn't going to get a blow job now.

"It's about damn time auntie Alice got here." Karmen's voice carried across the room.

"Oh girl, you are going to get it now. Karmen is on the rampage about you not hauling your cookies to Weston sooner." Cora slipped off her stool and rounded the bar. "Out of my way, old man. I need a drink, and since you're only serving your chick, I need to get my own."

I slowly spun around and plastered yet another huge smile on my face. "Hi!" I yelled two octaves higher than I normally spoke. "You had a baby!"

She had one of those baby basket things at her feet, but I couldn't see inside. It was turned backward so all I could see was the blue canopy thing that had little airplanes all over it. I wasn't very good at the whole baby thing.

Karmen rolled her eyes. "How nice of you to notice."

"Told ya. Salty as hell." Cora cleared her throat. "I'm gonna make some french fries. You think you could come over here and throw some of that salty attitude all over them?"

Wrecker chuckled behind me, and Nikki snorted.

"You're cut out of being his godmother."

Cora scoffed. "You take that away ten times a day. I really don't think you'll actually do it."

"Do godmothers really do anything besides spoil the shit out of the kid and then send him home?" Nikki whispered. "Sounds like you got out of a pretty expensive deal."

"They do more than that," Karmen insisted. "If Nickel and I both die, you have to take care of Cole."

"All three of us? Together?" I asked. "So, we're like lesbian mothers raising your kid in the wild?"

Karmen lifted up the carrier thing. "I don't know what I was thinking picking you three. I should have just picked Wren. She takes it much more serious than you guys." She set the carrier on the couch and pushed back the canopy. "Are you going to come see him or are you actually giving up your godmother rights?"

I hopped off my stool and strolled over to the couch. "Fair warning, I have zero baby experience. I was an only child, and I had no cousins." I could count on one hand the amount of times I had held a baby in my arms. "Even my cabbage patch doll died a miserable death in the garbage truck. I had stuck her in there thinking she needed to take a nap since it was dark in there. I had forgotten it was garbage day." I signed a cross over my chest and kissed my fingers. "Rest in peace, Princess Cow Turtle."

Karmen unbuckled Cole from the car seat and lifted him up into her arms. "You named your doll Princess Cow Turtle?"

I nodded and got the first glimpse of Cole. "Oh, he's sure cute, even with that huge string of drool hanging from his mouth."

"Mommy really needs to get some new friends," she whispered. "You up for holding him?"

"You just have to promise not to set him down in the garbage can," Cora called. "We couldn't have anything tragic happen to Cole like it did for poor Princess Cow Turtle."

I gently grabbed Cole from Karmen and cradled him in my arms. "Oh, I don't think I could ever put this little guy down," I cooed. He had dark mahogany hair like Karmen, Nickel's nose, and the cutest little outfit I have ever seen before. His eyes were closed, and he looked so peaceful. "How is he still sleeping?"

"He eats, sleeps, and poops, Alice. I changed and fed him before I came over, so all he has to do right now is sleep and grow."

"I need to be a baby," Nikki called. "Sounds like one hell of a life."

"Can I sit down with him?" I asked. I was terrified to walk with him, let alone lower myself onto the couch.

Karmen motioned to the couch. "Yeah, just keep his head supported."

"Five minutes," Pipe called.

"Five minutes for what?" Nickel asked. He walked into the clubhouse with dark blue bag on his shoulder and pushing a stroller. He looked like a badass biker dad. Cole was going to be one of the coolest kids in school with having parents like Karmen and Nickel.

"Freak had fifteen minutes to go to the liquor store or he would have to clean Wrecker's bike," Pipe laughed.

"That's a shitty deal. You've been riding back and forth to Kales Corners so I'm sure she's just plastered full of bugs." Nickel dropped the bag at Karmen's feet and parked the stroller by the door. "You really think we need to bring the stroller in with us no matter where we go?" he asked Karmen.

"I have no idea. I just keep reading that we should be prepared for anything to happen. Who knows when I might need the stroller." Karmen sat down next to me and gave a little wave to sleeping Cole. "I think he finally recognizes me, though that maybe all in my head. He seems happy to see me all the time."

"I bet it's gas," Cora snickered.

"And he's sleeping so I'm not sure how you are measuring the fact that he recognizes you," Nikki snickered.

"Taken away," Karmen hollered.

"Shh," I hushed. I didn't want Cole to wake up because then I had no idea what to do with him. When he was a sleeping log in my arms, I could handle him.

"Sleep forever, little boy." Or at least until he was old enough to walk.

"So," Karmen drawled. "Where have you been? I thought for sure you would be here with cowbells on the day Cole was born."

I kept my eyes on Cole. "I was busy with a couple of things."

"Things like getting it on with Wrecker," Nikki snickered.

"Shut. Up," Karmen said, astounded. "You're getting it on with the beard?"

I wasn't the only one who was rather taken aback with his beard. "Um, yeah." Oh, how I wish Karmen would have been here when I went over this with Nikki and Cora.

"Well, hot damn. You landed yourself a president, girlfriend." Karmen held her hand up for me to high five, but I was too terrified to move either of my hands.

"Uh, raincheck on the high five 'til I give away your baby."

"Keep him away from garbage cans," Cora called again. She was on a damn roll today.

"So what else has been going on with you?"

I rolled my eyes. They were all acting like they hadn't seen me in months when it had actually only been a couple of weeks. "Working and uh, hanging out with Wrecker."

"Made it!" Freak blew into the clubhouse with three bags on each wrist and a huge smile on his face. "Thirty seconds to spare."

"What is he talking about?" Karmen whispered.

"Wrecker was being a dick to him, but for some odd reason, he enjoyed it." Cole gave a little whimper, and I froze, not knowing what to do.

Karmen laughed. "Breathe, Alice. He's just getting comfy."

"As long as he stays asleep, I'll be fine." Once this guy cracked open his eyes, he was going straight back to his momma. I was getting anxiety from holding his sleeping little body. I would probably pass out when he woke up. I was rather pathetic when it came to babies. They were completely dependent on me, and let's be honest here, I was not one to rely on for anything besides pouring a strong drink.

Wrecker walked over to the couch and looked down at me. "You good?"

That was a tough question. For the moment, I was good, but that could all change in a split second. "Uh, I think for now I am. You want a baby?" *Please say yes.*

He chuckled and shook his head. "I'm good, babe. I gotta grab some shit and talk to the guys."

He was going to leave me alone. *Crap.* But why was it scary to be left alone? These were my friends. *Deep breath, Alice.* "Okie dokie. I'll be right here sitting like a statue, hoping this baby doesn't wake up."

He leaned down and pressed a kiss to my forehead. "Holler if you need me, babe. I won't be far," he whispered.

I nodded and tried not to let the tears that were clogging my throat seep out. "'Kay."

Wrecker headed down the hallway that led to all the guys' bedrooms.

I sniffled and looked down at Cole.

"Are you crying?" Karmen whispered.

Shit. Shitshitshitshitshitshit. "Uh, no. Of course not. I just have something in my eye." I tried to move my hand to wipe my face, but I didn't know how to hold Cole with just one arm. Man, I sure was a rookie when it came to this baby stuff.

"Girl Gang assemble," Karmen called.

"Wait, what?" I mumbled.

Cora muttered under her breath, and Nikki clapped her hands together like a happy seal. "I love when we do this. Though normally, we only do it when we're drinking so now that we actually have something to talk about, I am *uber* excited."

Cora sat down in the chair opposite the couch, and Nikki sat on the other side of me. "I feel like we should call Wren because she should be put through this torture too," Cora mumbled.

"Torture?" Karmen glared at Cora.

She held up her hands and shrugged. "Hey, hey. So, torture might be a bit too harsh." She pulled out her phone. "Perhaps Wren should be a part of this *amazing...*thing." She wrinkled her nose and looked down at her phone.

"Sometimes, I wonder if you even have a heart, Cora," Nikki laughed.

"I do," Cora mumbled. "It's black and matches my soul."

Karmen clapped her hands twice. "Can we please focus on Alice."

"We really don't need to focus on me." I nodded my head down at Cole. "We should all be focused on this little potato right here."

Nikki pursed her lips. "Uh, potato?"

Cora cracked up laughing. "Oh, my God," she wheezed. "I have never seen a person more uncomfortable around a baby before."

Karmen gently lifted Cole from my arms and sat back in the couch with him laid out on her chest. "Spill the beans, woman," she ordered. "I wanna know how Wrecker managed to fall into your bed without any of us having the slightest clue about it."

Cora raised her hand. "I didn't know it was going on, but I'm not as shocked as you two are. She's hot in that crazy kind of way, and Wrecker is a good-looking guy. It's really not crazy at all that they ended up together. Total yin and yang."

"That is the smartest thing I have ever heard you say." Nikki held her hand up. "Across the room high five." Cora raised her hand, and they pretended to high five.

"No, no, no. I seriously can't be the only one who is quite honestly blown away by this. I just need to know how this happened. Why did it happen? Do you actually want it to be happening? That man is the complete opposite of you, Alice."

I shifted uncomfortably on the couch. If I called for Wrecker right now, I knew he would come running, but that would just cause more problems with Nikki, Karmen, and Cora. "I don't know, Karmen. He came over, and now he just keeps coming over."

She rolled her eyes. "I am going to need a ton more information than that."

"I already found out that she likes the beard thing when they're kissing. That was the thing I was massively curious about."

"I wanna know how it feels on *other* parts." Cora wiggled her eyebrows. "I know I'm not the only one thinking that."

I turned around to look at the bar. "I'm gonna make a round of drinks. Everyone want one?" I asked.

A chorus of "yes" went up, and I walked behind the bar.

"Do you like him?" Karmen asked.

I grabbed four glasses and filled them halfway with ice. "I think liking someone is kind of a necessity to want to spend time with them in and out of bed."

"Not true," Cora yelled. "I would much prefer boinking a guy I didn't know than do it with a guy I have to see every day."

"That's just because you haven't met a guy you want to hang out with. You need to get out of the club life and see what else there is out in the world." Karmen wagged her finger at Cora.

"Says the woman who is fully immersed in the club life. The problem with the club guys is they are all bossy assholes when not in bed."

I grabbed the bottle of champagne and worked on pulling out the cork. "I told Wrecker I only have to listen to him when I don't have clothes on."

"And what did he say to that?" Nikki laughed.

I tilted my head to the side. "I think he just laughed."

"That mountain of a man knows how to laugh?" Karmen shook her head. "That is something I am going to have to see for myself."

"I'm sure with Alice around, he's always laughing," Cora quipped.

I filled each glass more than halfway with champagne then added a splash of OJ. "I've been known to crack a joke or two." My whole life seemed to be a joke. But lately, the jokes hadn't had the same zing to them. "Come get your drinks, bitches."

"Bring me mine. I don't want to wake up Cole."

I grabbed Karmen's and left the other two on the bar. "So, you two bitches have to get your own. You guys didn't push a baby out of your hoo-ha last I checked."

"I got you, girl," Cora told Nikki. "I see how it is around here now."

"So, is that all we assembled for?" Nikki asked.

"Something is different about Alice." Karmen tapped her finger to her chin and looked up at me.

"Yeah, I haven't had a drink yet and you're hindering that by not taking yours out of my hand." I moved her drink closer to her. "Take the damn thing, woman."

She shook her head. "Nope, that isn't it."

I rolled my eyes and set her glass on the beat-up coffee table. "Can we move on from me, hmm?" I plopped down on the couch and kicked my feet up. "If I'm the most exciting thing going on in your lives, then we really need to do something to shake that shit up."

Nikki grabbed the drink Cora held out to her. "She popped a baby out of her vajayjay, and I've been decorating my house. I really don't know what Cora does all day."

"Oh, you guys are taking an interest in me now? How nice."

We all waited for her to tell us what she did. It really was a mystery. She didn't have a job, and she seemed to always be locked away in her room at the clubhouse.

"You sell tiny statues of elephants."

Cora blinked slowly. "Say what?"

I shrugged and took a swig of my drink. "Hey, it was the first thing that popped into my head."

"Do you actually use logic when you open your mouth, or just let it fly?"

"Oh, oh. I know what you do," Nikki sat forward on the couch. "You're one of those sex operators. You know, the ones that can get a guy off with only talking to them."

Cora pointed her finger at Nikki. "Completely wrong, but much more believable than selling elephants."

"*Statues* of elephants. Not actual elephants," I clarified.

"Well, that makes all the difference in the world," Karmen laughed.

"So, we know you're not a phone sex operator or elephant smuggler. Spill the beans, woman," Nikki insisted.

"Statues," I mumbled.

"I'm an editor."

We all stared at Cora.

For a long time.

"You just blew my mind," Karmen whispered.

"When you say editor, what exactly do you mean?" Nikki asked.

"People send me their manuscripts, I read them over, make notes of changes and shit, then send it back to them," Cora explained.

I turned to Nikki. "How is it that none of us knew this?"

"'Cause we're shitty friends," Karmen cried.

Nikki and I both shifted away from Karmen. "Why is she crying?" I whispered.

"I think this is her hormones out of whack. Pipe told me yesterday Nickel has no idea what to do with her." We both took a sip of our drinks and stared at Karmen.

I wasn't good at dealing with people's emotions. To me, the best way to deal with Karmen freaking out was pouring her another drink and possibly ordering a pizza.

"Uh, you don't have to cry 'cause you didn't know what I did for work. It's not anything we've talked about before so you're all good." Cora clicked her tongue and winked at Karmen. "Dry your weird ass tears and drink your drink. You're going to scare your baby."

My eyes darted to Cole, thankful he was still fast asleep even though his mom was on a weird emotional trip right now.

"Oh, what the hell? I thought she was getting better." Nickel walked into the clubhouse and grabbed Cole from Karmen. "Baby, what the hell are you crying about now?"

Karmen waved her hand at him. "I don't really know. We were talking and then Cora told us what she did for work and then I started crying."

"What the hell does she do for work that it would make you cry?" he demanded.

"Not a phone sex operator or elephant smuggler."

For Christ's sake, I was never going to live this one down. "Statues," I repeated.

Nickel looked even more confused now. "So, what the hell does she do if not that shit?"

"I'm an editor."

Nickel looked her up and down. "The elephants are more believable."

Cora threw her head back laughing. "Is it the tattoo covered arms or my shitty personality?"

"Both," we all said in unison.

Cora daintily crossed her legs and held her glass up. "I love surprising the hell out of you fuckers."

"What do you edit?" Nickel asked as he swayed back and forth, rocking Cole. Being a parent came natural to him, which was another surprise.

"Books, jackass. And I make damn good money too."

"Who makes good money?" Wrecker called. He walked over to the bar and grabbed the glass of water I had abandoned.

"Cora. She edits books," Nikki chirped.

"And before anyone says it, isn't it surprising she isn't a phone sex operator or smuggling elephants?" I drawled.

"Elephants is more believable. And if you make damn good money, why the hell aren't we charging you rent?" Wrecker grabbed the container of orange juice and splashed some into his cup.

"'Cause I'm not here because I want to be. I'm forced to be here because my brother is an idiot."

Nickel snickered. "Now, that's the damn truth."

Karmen reached back and socked him in the stomach. "It's still her brother, dumbass."

Cora waved her hand. "Really, it's okay. I don't live in some fantasy world where I think my brother is some hero. He's a dumbass and has messed up a lot of people's lives. Hopefully, he can fix shit before he gets his head blown off," she said matter-of-factly.

"We're getting it fixed." Wrecker drained his glass and set it on the bar. "You ready for that tour, babe?"

Butterflies flitted in my stomach, and goosebumps ran up my arms. "I guess I'd be down for that."

Karmen reached for the bag Nickel had set at her feet. "What does she need a tour for? Down the hallway is the bedrooms, and through that door is a big ass garage. Tour done."

"Baby," Nickel called as he wiggled his eyebrows.

Recognition dawned on her face. "Oh. That kind of tour. Yeah, totally give her the tour. I got my tour from Pipe, though."

"Baby," Nickel said again.

She swatted her hand at him. "You know I didn't mean that kind of tour. My tour was this is the bar, sit down and drink until Nickel comes back."

"That's when you earned the nickname Captain," Pipe called.

Karmen sighed. "Good times."

"Babe," Wrecker called.

I knew I had been nervous to hang out with the girls, but now that we were here, it wasn't that bad. "Coming."

He reached for my hand when I got near and tugged me down the dark hallway. "You okay?"

"Um, I think so. Things got a little hairy with all the questioning, but I'm good."

We walked to the end of the hallway then hooked a right. "We're the last door on the left. Cora took over my old room, and I moved down here."

"Whose room was it before?"

He pulled his keys out of his pocket and jabbed one into the door handle. "No one's. We just used it to store random shit." He pushed open the door and motioned for me to walk in.

He flipped on the light switch, and I was surprised as hell for the second time today. "It's huge."

He chuckled behind me, and I heard the door shut. He flipped the lock and wrapped his arms around me. "That's always nice to hear come out of your mouth."

"I'm talking about your room, Wrecker. Not about what's in your pants."

He brushed my hair to the side and pressed his lips to my ear. "I already know you think that's huge, babe."

"You would remember that."

He pressed a kiss to my ear. "You say a lot of shit so I try to remember the important stuff."

I didn't have much else to say. All I could do was look at his room in awe. "Did we step into another dimension?" The difference from the clubhouse to Wrecker's room was unbelievable.

The walls were painted a rich, dark brown, and the floor was covered in lush beige carpet that made me want to slip my shoes off and sink my toes into it. His king-sized bed was pressed up against the far wall with a deep, dark black comforter laid over it. "Is that a fireplace?" I gasped.

"Just an electric one, babe. The heat is shit in the winter this far out from the common room. That was why no one ever took this room."

I looked over my shoulder at him. "Yet you gave your room up for Cora so she wouldn't have to sleep here."

He shrugged and pushed me further into the room. "It's nice being away from the guys a bit and sleeping with an extra blanket on really isn't that big of a deal."

"Mmmhmm, is that how you are going to play it off?" Wrecker may be all tough and gruff, but I knew underneath all those muscles and beard, he was a good man.

"How about we get a little silence, babe?"

"Oh, so you can avoid talking about stuff but I can't?"

He wrapped me up in his arms and threaded his fingers in my hair. He gently tugged, and I tipped my head back to look up at him. "I'm not avoiding anything, babe."

I rested my hands on his shoulders. "You're a good man, Wrecker."

"That's an unpopular opinion, Alice."

"It may be unpopular, but it's my opinion. I'm right, too."

He shook his head. "You can believe whatever you want inside that pretty head, babe, but I know a few people who would argue with you."

I cleared my throat. "You know what I say? People who don't believe in you aren't worth your time. Also, people who say pizza isn't a breakfast food aren't worth your time. You really don't need that kind of negativity in your life."

"So, I let you eat pizza for breakfast this morning and that makes me a good man?" he laughed.

"I mean, there's more to it, but that's a good place to start." He lifted me up and walked toward the bed. "Wait!"

His steps faltered, and his arms squeezed tightly around me. "What is it?"

"Can we go to the couch?" I pointed over his shoulder at the large couch that was in front of the fireplace. "I kind of wanted to do something for you."

"For me?" he asked

I nodded. "Yep, but I'm not going to tell you what it is. You need to go sit on the couch and let me go."

"Not really into having you far away from me right now, babe."

There went the damn butterflies again. "I promise I'm not going anywhere. Just let me down and go sit."

His brow furrowed, but he let me down. "Your ass better be following right behind me."

Even when I was trying to be bossy, he had to throw some assiness at me. I pushed on his shoulder and nodded to the couch. "Go." He moved to go sit on the couch, and I pulled my shirt over my head. "Oh, and no turning around." He shook his head, but thankfully listened.

I had changed my mind about his blow job when he had whispered to me that he was always close by. Then he had held my hand while we walked down the hallway. He was racking up all sorts of blow job points. I kicked off my shoes, unbuttoned my pants, and dropped them to the floor.

"Where the hell are you?" The low timber of his voice sent a shiver up my back.

I reached behind me and unhooked my bra. "Hold your horses, man." I took a deep breath and moved to the couch. "Wait!"

"Jesus Christ, woman. What now? I heard your damn clothes hit the floor and my dick is rock hard. There really isn't much more to wait for."

"Uh, you need to take your clothes off. I didn't factor that into my plan before." Having him stand up after he saw me was totally going to kill the flow of what I had envisioned in my mind. "But don't turn around. Take off your clothes and stay facing the fireplace."

He shook his head but stood up. He yanked his shirt off and tossed it over his head at me.

"Hey," I protested when it landed on my head. I yanked it off and saw him bent over. "Whatcha doing there?" I moved closer to the couch to see his jeans strain against his tight ass.

"About to say fuck whatever plan you having going on in your head and just fuck the shit out of you."

"What?" I squawked. "You can't do that." I had this planned out in my head, and dammit, it was going to go the way I wanted it to.

He stood up, unbutton his pants and dropped them around his ankles. He held his arms out with his palms up. "Now what, babe?"

The urge to pull out my phone and take a picture was strong. "Uh, picture time?"

He lowered his hands and shook his head. "Dick hard as a goddamn rock and you want to take pictures. You're killing me here."

"It's a good photo op," I whispered. "But, since you don't want to do that, you can sit back down and I can resume my master plan."

He sat down on the couch and spread his arms out on the back. "You better not be grabbing a camera, woman. I'll lay you across my lap and spank that lush ass of yours."

"Lush? That sounds kind of sexy."

"You are sexy, Woman. Now get your ass over here."

So bossy. But it was hot, and it turned me on even though it would be a cold day in Hell that I would admit that to him.

I walked the few steps to the couch. "Close your eyes."

"Closed," he growled.

I was walking a thin line telling him what to do, but I knew it was all going to pay off in the end. "Good boy."

"Alice."

Yep, he was getting pissed.

I stood in front of him and took in the gloriousness of his muscled thighs and huge dick that was standing at attention, waiting for me. "Sweet sticky molasses."

"Babe, you need to ride it or suck it."

I ignored his impatient tone. "Spread your legs."

He cocked open his legs, and I knelt between them. I rested my hands on his thighs, and a soft moan fell from my lips.

I lowered my head and pressed a kiss to the tip of his penis.

"Fuck. Yes. I've been dreaming of your mouth on my dick." His eyes were open, and he looked like he wanted to devour me.

I leaned back and smiled. "Dreams do come true, Mr. President," I whispered. I wrapped my hand around the base cock and squeezed.

"You look hot as fuck with my dick in your hand."

"Just wait and see what else I plan to do."

*

CHAPTER 13

WRECKER

Her mouth was like a hot, wet vise on my dick. She moved her mouth up and twisted her hand down. Over and over. The soft mewling that came from her throat was almost as good as the feel of her mouth.

I threaded my fingers though her hair, gripping her scalp, and pulled her up and down. "Fuck yeah, babe."

Her hand that wasn't on my dick swept up my leg and onto my chest. Her nails dug into my pecs, and the sharp bite of pain made me close my eyes and drop my head back. A low moan rumbled from my chest, and my balls tightened as she sucked hard while her hand twisted up.

"I'm gonna come, babe," I strangled out.

She doubled her efforts instead of shrinking away. My fingers gripped her scalp, and my hips lifted off the couch as I poured my cum down her throat. I felt her swallow around my dick as I was coming down from the best blow job of my life. "Son of a bitch," I breathed out.

She slid her mouth down on my dick one last time, then pulled off with a loud pop. She wiped the corners of her mouth and sat back on her heels. She looked up at me, and I had no fucking clue what to say. This woman who was always the life of the party was actually broken inside, and I had been the one she chose to share that with. I knew more about her than anyone out in that room.

"Okay?"

Okay? Fucking Christ. That had been everything but okay. "Fucking amazing."

A huge smile spread across her lips. "Yeah?"

Jesus. She had to have known by how hard I just came that I wasn't shitting her. I grabbed her under her arms and lifted her onto my lap. My dick was already rebounding from the workout she had just given it. "The fact that my dick is ready to go again should show you just how amazing that was."

She rested her hands on my shoulders and sighed. "That was way better than I imagined it would be. I figured it would be hot as hell, but I should have known with you, everything is always fifty gazillion times better."

My hands palmed her ass, and I lifted her slightly 'til her sweet pussy was lined up with my dick. "Gonna fuck you now, babe."

She slowly sunk down on my dick, and her eyes closed. "I'm not going to argue with you on that, Mr. President," she whispered.

"Move," I growled. She was so fucking hot and wet that my dick was ready to fucking explode again. I didn't know how the hell she did it, but she drove me fucking insane.

She used her hand on my shoulders to lift up on her knees, then she slowly slid back down. "I'm going to do this for the rest of my life," she sighed.

"Fuck me?" I grunted. I had never been one to talk so much during sex, but with Alice, holding a conversation while my dick was buried inside her was something that happened.

"Yes," she moaned.

"Babe, I love fucking you, but you gotta give me a break every now and then."

She leaned in and pressed a hot, greedy kiss against my lips. "Breaks are for wussies, not bad ass biker presidents."

She was going to fucking kill me.

I jack-knifed off the couch with her legs wrapped around me, my dick still buried in her sweet pussy, and stalked over to the bed. "Then I guess I'm going to have to wear you out, babe." I planted a knee on the bed and laid her down.

She spread her legs and pulled them up to her chest, giving me a whole new angle to drive into her. "Don't stop," she moaned.

I smashed my lips down on her mouth, and my hips pounded into her. Our breathing was labored, and our moans mingled together. "So fucking good," I groaned against her lips. There was never going to be another woman like Alice. God broke the mold when he made her, and I was the lucky bastard who got to have her.

"Didn't plan on it," I growled. I sat back and looked down at her. Her dark, silky hair was spread out on the pillow, and her eyes were closed. Her bottom lip was pulled between her teeth, and her hands clenched the sheets.

My hands grabbed behind her knees and jacked her legs up even higher. I thrusted hard, making sure she would feel me everywhere. Alice didn't want me to stop, and I wanted her to remember who was inside her long after we were done.

Her pussy clenched around my dick, milking me. "Please, Wrecker," she moaned. "Harder."

I collapsed back down on top of her and planted my hands next to her head. "Fucking insatiable," I growled.

She wrapped her arms around my neck and pulled me close. "Only for you." She pressed her lips to mine, and I sucked on her bottom lip while she buried her fingers into my hair.

She threw her head back as she came around my dick and moaned long and hard. I pounded into her, needing to come while her pussy squeezed and milked my dick.

"Alice," I shouted as I came again. Her fingers sifted through my hair, and her legs wrapped around me as I pumped my cum into her pussy.

"How does that get better every time?" she mused quietly.

I collapsed onto the bed, my legs tangled with hers, and sighed. "No fucking clue," I mumbled. She was right, though. I didn't know how it was possible, but I had just come even harder than I had when her lips were wrapped around my dick ten minutes ago.

We laid there, both of us panting. She ran her fingers through my beard and sighed.

"What are you thinking, babe?" I murmured.

"Nothing important," she whispered.

"You know you're going to tell me."

She shook her head. "No, I'm not."

"Hungry?" I asked.

"I'm always hungry, Wrecker."

"Then you're thinking about pizza."

She laughed and threaded her fingers through mine. Her other hand continued to pet my beard. "Do you ever comb this?"

"That's what you were thinking about?" I laughed.

"Well, no, but I was watching my hand and then I thought about how soft your beard is."

"I run my fingers through it in the morning."

She hummed under her breath.

"Now tell me what you were thinking about."

She rolled into me and pushed me onto my back. She rested her head on my shoulder and pressed her finger to my lips. "You talk too much."

Now that was the pot calling the fucking kettle black. "Wonder who I learned that from." I pressed a kiss to her finger and threaded my fingers through hers.

"What's your name?" she asked. "Like your real name."

"Really?" That's what she was thinking about?

"You know what? Never mind. I can just look at your driver's license and be disappointed quietly when you tell me it's Norbert or something like that."

"Damn, babe. You got me pegged. My name is Norbert."

Her jaw dropped, and she raised her head to look at me. "Seriously?"

I nodded.

"I don't believe you," she fired.

I shrugged. "Gotta take my word for it, babe."

"Um, nah I don't." She jumped off the bed and frantically looked around on the floor.

"What in the hell are you doing, woman?" Not that I didn't enjoy the view of her tits and pussy, but I liked it better when she was lying next to me.

She pointed her hand at me and snapped her fingers. "By the couch." She dove over the back of the couch and fell to the floor.

"Woman, what in the hell?" I couldn't see her but I could hear her scrambling around.

Her arm raised over the couch with my wallet in hand. "You tell me what your real name is, or I will forever call you Norbert. Even in front of you club dudes. You will forever be President Norbert."

"You're killing me, babe," I laughed. My name wasn't Norbert, but it was fucking funny watching her to try and figure it out. "There is nothing wrong with the name Norbert. It's what my mama called me."

"I fully believe you came out of the womb with a beard and a scowl on your face. I need to meet your mother to verify these things." She stood up in all her naked glory and clutched the wallet to her chest. "Now tell me your name before I open your wallet and find out myself."

"Does it matter what it is? I can't even remember the last time someone has even called me it. Even my sister calls me Wrecker."

She tilted her head to the side. "You have a sister?"

"Yea, and before your brain starts going crazy, she is not the bearded woman."

She sputtered, trying to hold back her laughter. "My mind didn't even go there, but now that you said that, I'm going to have to meet her when I meet your mom to verify that neither of them have beards."

"Mom's dead, babe, and my sister and I don't talk much."

Her face fell. "Shit. I'm sorry."

I shook my head. "Ain't nothing to be sorry and sad about. Now toss me the wallet."

She shook her head. "Nope. Not until you tell me your name."

I rolled my eyes and dropped my head to the pillow. "Cary."

"Come again?"

I lifted my head and looked at her. "My fucking name is Cary, babe."

She opened my wallet and studied my license. "Well, I'll be damned." She looked up at me. "Your name really is Cary."

"Now she listens to me."

She looked back down at my wallet. "Bloom? Cary Bloom is your name?" The disbelief in her voice was almost laughable. "You do not look like a Cary Bloom, Wrecker."

"Why you think people only know me as Wrecker?"

She tossed the wallet onto the couch and catapulted herself back onto the bed. "I'm not calling you Cary. You'd have to shave the beard and start selling insurance."

I wrapped her in my arms and pulled her onto my chest. "Two things that are never going to fucking happen, babe."

She tugged on my beard and smiled. "That is good to know, Mr. President."

"I like that a hell of a lot better than Cary," I chuckled.

She pressed a finger to my lips. "We shall never speak of this moment again."

I nipped at her finger, and she squealed playfully. "So, that was all you were thinking about, babe?"

Her eyes got serious, and she shook her head. "I lied before."

Oh hell. "Yeah? Tell me."

She swallowed hard and looked to the side. "I really was wondering if you think they would deliver pizza to your room so I didn't have to put pants on."

*

CHAPTER 14

ALICE

"I have to work in the morning."

Wrecker cracked open one eye. "No."

Uh, yeah. I needed to pay my rent, and unfortunately, I wasn't getting paid to lie in bed with Wrecker at the clubhouse. "We need to go now or in the morning."

"What time do you work?" he asked sleepily. He had just fucked me again for the third time, and we were both exhausted. I had just woken up from our two-hour nap and had been studying his handsome face when I remembered there was a world outside of the bed we were lying in.

"Eight."

He groaned. "That means we would have to leave at six in the morning to get you there in time."

It would be more like five-thirty. "Um, yeah."

"What time is it right now?"

I glanced at the clock he had next to the bed. "Half past seven."

"We leave now, then. I'll get you in bed before ten so you can get a full night's sleep."

I laughed. I couldn't remember the last time I had a full, good night's sleep. Normally, it took copious amounts of booze to make me pass out without waking up in the middle of the night. Though the night prior in the hotel, Wrecker had worn me out to the point where booze wasn't needed for me to pass out.

"You know, we came here so I could hang out with my girls, and instead, you kept me locked away in your room all day."

"We can come next weekend," he mumbled.

"Are you really that tired?" I giggled.

He opened both of his eyes and looked up at me. "Your couch at your house is shit, babe. I'm enjoying the feel of my bed before I'm back on that thing."

"Orrr," I drawled. "You can just sleep in my bed with me when you come over."

"I plan on being there a lot."

The butterflies in my stomach fluttered again. I wasn't ever going to get used to the sweetness that came out of his mouth at random times. "Well, then I guess you can sleep in bed with me."

He threw back the covers and stretched his arms over his head. "Let's hit the road then, babe."

"Uh, maybe we should get dressed first."

He looked at my chest covered in his shirt he had been wearing earlier. It was three sizes too big on me, and it hung almost to my knees. It smelt like him, though, and I didn't want to take it off. I was most certainly also going to steal it when he wasn't looking. "Fallen Lords looks good on you, babe."

"You guys totally need to get some girl shirts made up. I would totally wear them all the time."

"Yeah?"

I nodded and rocked up onto my knees to press a kiss to his lips. "Yeah, I would."

"I'll see if I can make that happen. I'm sure the other chicks would be down with that, too."

"All of them except for Cora. I'll take the ones that you make for her."

"Put some pants on and let's head out, babe."

I scooted out of bed and looked over my shoulder at Wrecker. "So, does that mean I can keep this shirt? I could sleep in it every night."

He sat up and rubbed the sleep out of his eye. "It's yours, babe. Just don't start stealing all of my shirts."

I stood up and felt the shirt fall against my thighs. "As much as I would love to do that, I know that they would all end up looking like dresses on me." I hiked the shirt up and knotted the end. "That should do for now."

Wrecker stood up and walked over to the dresser along the wall next to the fireplace. He took out a pair of pants and pulled them on.

I found my jeans in a pile next to the bed, and we both got dressed in silence. He pulled a comb through his hair and tossed it to me. "I think you look hot as fuck right now, babe, but it looks like I fucked the hell out of you, and as much as I like that, I'm the only one who needs to know that."

"Can I comb your beard?" I pulled the comb through my hair a couple of times and walked up to Wrecker.

"You're serious right now?"

I nodded. "As a heart attack. I think it would feel nice to have my beard played with all the time. I know it's nice when someone plays with my hair."

"Who the hell plays with your hair?" he demanded.

"Uh, my hair dresser? I purposely go there with the intention of getting a nice head massage and have her diddle with my hair."

"Don't say diddle, babe. Not when you're talking about your hair chick."

I propped my hands on my hips. "Can I comb your beard or not? It's an easy question."

"Only if you let me pet your pussy later."

Now he was the one surprising the hell out of me with the things coming out of his mouth. "I don't have any hair down there to play with." Thank God for waxing. Could you imagine a guy asking if he could comb a chick's beaver? Or pet it? Though Wrecker had just told me he planned on petting my beaver. "And who asks if they can pet someone's beaver?"

"Beaver?" he chuckled. "I prefer pussy."

I smirked. "Yeah, you do." I held the comb up to his beard. "I'm gonna do it."

"Pretty sure I can't stop you so just go for it, babe, so we can get on the road."

I pulled the comb through his hair and sighed. "Look how fluffy it's getting."

He looked down at his beard and tugged the comb out of my hand. "And that is why you don't comb my beard." He tossed the comb on the dresser and gathered his beard in his hand. He pulled it down a few times, then patted it into submission. "Say bye to your girls and let's hit the road."

"Can we stop for pizza and beer?"

He rolled his eyes and grabbed his cut from off the back of the couch. "Maybe tacos and beer?"

I clenched my hand to my chest and felt the tears start to well. "You have hit on my second favorite food combination, though you could have said tacos and margaritas and I would have been excited."

He pulled on his cut and reached onto the couch for his wallet. "Good. Tacos, and then home."

"And margaritas," I called. I slipped my shoes on and tied them.

We walked out into the common room holding hands, and I'm sure I had a goofy-ass smile plastered on my face.

"Well, well. They finally surface." Brinks was sitting at one of the poker tables, and Freak was perched on the other side.

"What the hell are you two doing?" Wrecker asked.

"Everyone went to the fucking movies to see the new dinosaur movie, and I drew the short straw to have to stay here with Freak," Brinks complained. He tossed a card across the table and turned over one in front of him.

"What are you guys playing?" I asked.

"War." They said in unison.

"We're heading out. Tell Pipe I'll call him in a couple days and that we'll be back this coming weekend." Wrecker wrapped his arm around my shoulders and pulled me close.

"Try not to have too much fun," I called. We walked out the front door, straight to Wrecker's bike.

"You really want tacos, babe?" He handed me my helmet, and I set it on my head.

"I never joke about tacos, Wrecker."

He chuckled and threw a leg over his bike. "Tacos it is, then."

I climbed on behind him and wrapped my arms around his waist. "I promise to make it up to you when we get home if you stop for tacos."

He started the bike and revved the engine. "I know just the place, babe."

He fed me tacos.

Took me home.

I showed my appreciation for the tacos. Twice.

He got to sleep in my bed.

*

Chapter 15

Wrecker

"Nothing is happening."

"Come again?"

"No one is talking to her. She hasn't made any friends, and they all give her a wide berth. It's like they all know who she is but they haven't called her on it."

Son of a bitch. I slammed my hand down on the kitchen counter. "Have you talked to her? Did you tip them off that she's with the Lords?" I demanded.

"Dude, I haven't even talked to her. I always sit in a section that isn't hers and my eyes don't linger on her for more than a second. There isn't a way in hell that they would know who I am or who she is."

I turned around and leaned against the counter. Alice was due home any minute, and I was looking forward to surprising her with the present I had for her in the living room. Now, I was pissed off that things weren't going how they should with Raven.

"I'm not there, Boink, so you gotta explain more. Do I need to pull her?" I didn't want anything to happen to Raven. We didn't talk often, but she was still my sister. When I needed to drop someone into The Ultra, I knew she would be perfect. She was single, had no kids, and had been a waitress since she was fifteen. But the thing that made her the perfect fit was the fact I knew she could handle herself.

"It doesn't feel right, Wrecker. They haven't done anything to her, but I know something is about to go down."

"But how do you know that if you haven't talked to her?" I demanded.

"Well, you told me not to talk to her so I'm going off of gut feeling here. I can't tell you what or why, but *something is* going to happen."

Fuck.

FUCK!

"You need me there now?" I hated not knowing what to do. This was why I wanted to be the one there with Raven. Now, I had to rely on Boink to keep her safe.

"Let me talk to her. Make sure she feels the same shit brewing that I do."

"Well, hopefully whatever the hell you are feeling is way off, Boink. We need this to work or I don't know how else we are going to fix the shit storm we're in the middle of."

Boink sighed. "She's off tonight. I'm going to head over to her place and talk with her."

"Make sure no one fucking sees you, Boink. If our cover isn't blown, you going over there might be the thing to blow it up."

"I got it. I'll let you know when I find anything out."

"The second you hear anything, you call me. Don't fuck this up any more than it is, Boink." I ended the called and tossed it on the counter.

"Fuck!" God dammit.

I heard Alice's keys in the door and took a deep breath. I was going to have to deal with the mess Raven was in later. Right now, there wasn't anything I could do until Boink told me more. Once he met with Raven, she would be able to tell him if everything was going south.

Alice walked through the door with a big smile on her face. "Hey!"

"Hey, babe."

She dropped her purse on the floor by the door and kicked off her shoes. "You know, it's been almost two weeks since Bos and I got arrested, and he is still giving me shit about it? I mean, he me—" Her words died in her throat when her eyes landed on the couch. "Where did my couch go?"

"I got you a new one, babe. That thing was on its last leg."

"But it was my couch." Her eyes were glued to the spot where the new, plush couch sat.

"Just sit on this one, babe, and you'll change your tune really quick."

She shook her head. "I don't want to change my tune, Wrecker. That was my damn couch. It was my mother's couch before she went to go live in the nursing home. It was hers and then it was mine."

Fuck. I had messed up. Big time. "I didn't know, babe."

She looked up at me and glared. "You didn't know because you didn't ask. You just did whatever you wanted because you thought that was what was best."

"I was just trying to help, babe."

"Help? Who helps someone by buying them a couch? Helping is buying a cup of coffee or picking up someone's newspaper off their wet lawn and sticking it in their mailbox."

"I didn't know it was going to be such a big issue."

She threw her hands up in the air. "That's because you didn't ask, Wrecker. You just did whatever you wanted because that's how you operate."

"I can fix this, Alice." I had put her old couch in the garage. I had scheduled for it to be picked up tomorrow, but it was something I could easily cancel.

"But you shouldn't have to fix it if you would have run it by me before. This isn't your club where you make all the decisions and I'm just supposed to go along with them. It's my damn life, and that was my damn couch."

She stalked into the kitchen and whipped open the door to the liquor cabinet.

"What are you doing?" I demanded. We were in the middle of talking and she was going to make herself a drink?

She glared at me over her shoulder. "Giving the Pope a blow job. What the hell does it look like I'm doing?" She grabbed down the first bottle her hand touched and slammed it on the counter.

"It looks like instead of dealing with what's going on around you, you are getting drunk."

"Ding, ding, ding," she sang. "Hit the nail right on the head with that one, Mr. President."

"What the hell is going on, Alice?"

She opened the freezer, grabbed out an ice cube, and slammed it shut. "I'm making a drink. Then I'm going to figure out what you did with my couch, and then I'm going to get it back."

"It's in the garage."

She raised a hand over her head. "Great. Now I can just get drunk and sit on my couch."

"Babe, I'm not going to be able to move it by myself. I'm gonna have to have one of the guys come and help me."

She pulled a glass from the cabinet and dropped the ice into it. "No, you're not going to have to do that because you're not staying."

"What the hell are you talking about?"

She splashed the amber liquid into the glass and downed it in one gulp. "I wanna be alone, Wrecker. I can't be alone when you're constantly towering over me and telling me what to do."

"I don't tell you want to do, Alice."

She laughed and filled the glass again. "You're right. You don't tell me, you just fucking do it."

"Can we please have this conversation without you getting drunk?"

She shook her head. "Nope, not happening."

"You've gone almost two weeks without having a damn drink, and now something happens, something that is easily fixable, and you go back to drinking."

She laughed flatly. "I don't want fixing, Wrecker. I know that's what you think you're doing being here, but you can stop. I'm not interested. It was nice living in this little fantasy world with you for a bit, but I think it's time for you to go now."

"No."

"No, he says," she mumbled.

"I'm not trying to fix you. I'm not trying to give you some perfect little world, Alice."

"Then what the hell are you trying to do, then? Get in my pants? Mission accomplished. On to the next broken girl for you to fix."

"You're not even making any fucking sense right now."

She tapped her finger to her head. "It all makes sense up here."

"I can't talk to you when you're like this."

She held her arm up and pointed a finger at the door. "Good. Then leave." She grabbed her glass and tucked the bottle under her arm.

"Where the hell are you going?"

She walked out the front door and slammed it behind her.

Fucking Christ. I was just trying to do something nice. Her couch was so worn out that every time we sat on it, one of us always ended up getting poked by one or fifty springs.

I knew she was headed to the garage to sit on her couch. She also thought I was going to leave.

She thought wrong.

*

ALICE

Never trust a man who won't share his pickle with you. I couldn't help but laugh out loud. Momma had a hundred and one sayings she swore by, and each and every one of them was funny in their own right.

If it looks like a duck, quacks like a duck, then it's a duck. Or something along those lines. I could never remember that one correctly. Granted, most of Momma's sayings were common ones, but the sharing the pickle one always made me laugh.

I bit a huge hunk off my pickle and chewed slowly. It was a good thing I had a refrigerator in the garage. I was never going to have to go back in the house for as long as he decided to stay.

Though, I didn't have a bathroom. "Dammit." I could always drive to the gas station to take care of business if he stayed that long.

"I have never seen a bigger jar of pickles in my life."

I jumped up, pickle juice sloshing over the top of the jar. "Jumping reindeer. Why the hell are you sneaking up on me like that, man?" I dropped my half-eaten pickle back in the jar and set it at my feet.

"Babe, I knocked on the door. I figured you were ignoring me." He leaned against the doorframe and crossed his arms over his chest.

"Well, if I had known you were there, I would have been actively ignoring you."

He shook his head. "You're crazy amplifies when you drink."

I grabbed the half-drank bottle off the floor. "Why don't you join me, and we can be crazy together." The booze was in full effect now. My brain was screaming for him to get away from me, but yet, my mouth was telling him to stay.

"I'm surprised you haven't noticed."

I took a swig straight from the bottle and wiped my mouth with the back of my hand. "Noticed what?" I drawled.

"I don't drink."

I sat back and curled my lip. "Bullarky."

"I'll have a beer or a drink every now and then, but getting drunk hasn't happened in a long damn time."

I lifted up the bottle. "Don't worry, I'll make up for you the time." I squinted one eye and tried to figure out if what I had just said made sense. "I've lost my making sense."

He pushed off the door frame and moved over to the fridge. "I've never been in here before I showed the movers where to put the couch. I should start parking my bike in here."

"You'll have to go through the door. I can't find the damn opener." I held up my hand. "But wait, you can't come in here. This is my garage, and you were supposed to be gone." I slashed my hand through the air. "Way gone."

He grabbed a can of soda and shut the door. "You and I both know that isn't what you want."

I nodded. "Uh, 'tis to."

"If you wanted me gone, you wouldn't be talking to me right now."

"That's what it takes for you to leave?" I slurred. I drew a finger across my lips. "Zip, zip." There. That would show him I didn't want him here. "Silence."

He sat down on the end of the couch and popped open this soda. "You know I'm only interested in one kind of silence from you."

"Da nakey kind, and I can tell you right now, Cary...Cary whatever-your-last-name-is, you and I no longer have uglies to bump."

"Babe," he drawled.

He could give me that sexy smirk all day. It wasn't going to get my vagina any closer to his mega wiener. *Ha! Mega wiener.* It sounded like he was a brand-new Transformer. A dirty Transformer, but a Transformer nonetheless.

"Now you gotta tell me what the loopy smile is for."

I shook my head. "I'm not going to tell you I have now nicknamed you Mega Weiner." I closed one eye and pursed my lips. "Shit, I think I just told you." Gah, the booze was betraying me now.

"I'd love to spend one day inside that mind of yours."

I wagged a finger at him. "It's crowded up here, Beardilocks. It's a no for me."

He quietly looked at me. I hated when he looked at me. He could see things that I didn't want anyone to see. "I'm sorry about your couch, babe. If I had known it meant so much to you, I wouldn't have gotten you a new one."

I shrugged. "It's just a couch."

"That why you're sitting in your garage getting drunk while you sit on it because it's just a couch."

I took another swig from the bottle. I reached down and fished around for another pickle. "I was saying goodbye to it."

"With a jar of pickles."

"Momma wouldn't have it any other way. She loved pickles almost as much as she loved me." I found a big pickle and pulled it out. Juice ran down my arm, and I took a huge bite out of it. "She liked the spicy ones best."

"I wish I could have met her."

Gah, that went straight to my heart. She would have loved Wrecker. "She probably would have made some inappropriate comment about wanting to climb you like a tree." I set the bottle of booze next to the jar of pickles. "If you ever wondered where I got my weirdness from, it is a straight derivative from her."

"Derivative, babe?"

"I don't even know what that means, but it came out of my mouth." That about summed up me when I was drunk.

"Finish your pickle."

I shoved it into my mouth and crossed my eyes. "So dem bessy."

"Try saying that when your mouth isn't full."

I rolled my eyes and chewed. "You know, I hated this couch growing up. You think it's bad now, but it's been like that for a long damn time. She got it from the local thrift store so it was well worn by the time it graced our living room."

"I'll get it moved back into the living room tomorrow. I already texted Brinks and Freak to get their asses here right away in the morning."

"Uh, really?" Dammit, he was fixing it again. Fixing it when I was getting used to the idea of having a new couch. I didn't want to get rid of this one, but I wanted a new one in the living room. I picked at a loose string on the cushion. "I bet the new one doesn't have rips in it and springs that poke ya in the hoo-ha all of the time."

He sat back on the couch. "Gotta tell ya, babe. I took a nap on the new one before you got home. Felt like I was sleeping on a cloud."

I flicked the leftover pickle juices on my hand at him. "No fair. You got to be the first one to take a nap on my couch."

"It's going back to the store, babe."

"You know you're making an awful lot of work for people. It's not very nice."

"Well, what do you suggest I do? I don't want you mad at me for buying you that couch. I'll easily return it, and then we can move this back in."

Crap. How to tell him I wanted the couch even though I had thrown a major hissy fit. A hissy fit that I still felt was warranted, but a hissy fit nonetheless. "You're gonna make me say it, aren't you?"

"Seeing as you just ripped my head off for doing shit without talking to you, yeah, I'm going to make you say it."

"I hate you."

"Now who's not being nice?"

I rolled my eyes. "I want the couch, Wrecker. It's pretty, looks comfy, and I'm tired of my hoo-ha being poked all the time."

He raised one eyebrow.

"By the springs, Beardilocks. Not you."

"Good to know you haven't gotten sick of that yet."

That was something I was never going to get sick of. Even when the man had pissed me the hell off, I knew that wasn't something I wanted to give up. When I had told him to leave, I had only meant for the moment. Though, as you could see from the fact that he was sitting on Momma's couch, he didn't give me much of a moment to myself. "I did just give you the nickname Mega Wiener." Why did I keep telling him that? *Damn you, whiskey.*

"So, the couch stays, then?"

I nodded. "Both of them stay. I can always come in here if I wanna get my hoo-ha surprisingly poked and think of my momma."

"I'm going to assume you meant those as two separate thoughts."

I nodded. "You're catching on, Beardilocks."

"You wanna come over here now and tell me how your day was?"

He was sprawled out on the couch, his legs spread out in front of him, and his lap looked rather inviting. "Only if I get to pet your beard."

"I don't think I've ever said no to you doing that before, babe."

"You weren't a fan of the brushing I gave it the other day."

"Because you gave me a beard fro."

I giggled and shook my head. "It wasn't that bad."

"Come over here and tell me how bad it wasn't." He grabbed my hand and hauled me across the couch.

"I'm still mad at you," I complained as I straddled his waist and laid my hands on his shoulders.

"You can be mad at me while my dick is buried inside that sweet cunt of yours."

A tremor rocked my body, and I moaned as I dropped my forehead to his shoulder. "You can't say things like that," I whined. I wasn't going to have any control when he was around if he was so blunt and to the point.

"How about we do a different kind of talking."

"Silence?" I chirped.

"Silence, babe."

I pressed a kiss to his neck and sighed. He was going to piss me off. It was his nature to be bossy, and it was mine to fly off the handle and be absolutely ridiculous.

We seemed to work good together, though. He hadn't gone running for the hills yet.

*

CHAPTER 16

WRECKER

"Roll off and go get cleaned up, babe." I slapped her bare ass, and she didn't even move.

"Ugh, no. I'm just staying here all night. Just think of me as your blanket." She wrapped her arms around me and sighed. "We can't have sex like that, and then you expect me to do things like roll off of you."

"What if I order pizza?"

She slapped my arm. "Why do you toy with my emotions like this, Wrecker? You don't even understand the deep, dark, things I would do for a pizza."

"Pretty sure you just let me do two of those things to you." After she had let me fuck her on the couch, we had made it to the bed where she had worked out her pissy mood on me. I had to say that angry sex with Alice was something even more out of this world than anything we had done before.

She pressed a finger to my lips. "Shh...Only speak if you have the phone in your hand and you're ordering pizza."

I knocked her hand away. "I can't order pizza unless you slide your ass over."

She tipped her head back and squinted at me. "My mind can't decide if what you just said was hot or bossy as hell."

"Go with hot and scoot over."

She rolled over me like it was the hardest thing in the world to do. "Make sure you order extra pepperoni and banana peppers."

I grabbed my pants off the floor and tugged them on. "On your half. I don't want those damn yellow things all over my shit."

She blinked slowly. "Are we disagreeing about what to put on our pizza? Here I thought we were like a match made in Heaven because we both liked the same things."

I shook my head. "Banana peppers on pizza sucks, babe."

She clutched a hand to her chest. "Our whole relationship has been a lie up until this point."

"Fucking crazy," I mumbled under my breath. "Next thing you know, you'll be telling me to put pickles on the damn thing."

Her jaw dropped, and she jack-knifed off the bed. "Oh. My. God. You are a damn genius. I had forgotten they had cheeseburger pizza. I'm going to need you to order a large and tell 'em to put extra pickles on that sucker."

Like that shit was going to happen. "Uh, fuck no."

"It's amazing, Wrecker. You have to order. I promise that you won't regret it."

I combed my fingers through my beard and grabbed my phone. "You don't play fair, babe. You can't beg for something when you got your tits just hanging out. It's going to be a yes every time."

She cupped her breast in her hands and lifted them up. "You mean these old things?"

Fucking Christ. "Yeah. Put 'em away and go get cleaned up." I strutted out of the room before my dick decided that we needed to fuck her again.

I ordered the pizza, grabbed a couple of sodas from the fridge, and headed back down the hallway to the bathroom. "Babe, pizza is gonna be here in half an hour. You wanna watch a movie?" I pushed open the door, and steam rolled out from over the shower curtain.

"What's that?" she called.

"Movie and a pizza?"

She pulled back the curtain, and my dick stood at attention. Damn this woman for flashing her tits at me all the time. It had become a passing thing with her. "Yeah. I wanna test out the new couch even though you took a nap on it today."

"That was your own fault for keeping me up last night. I'm old and can't seem to keep up with you."

"You're full of shit. You were the one who woke me up in the middle of the night with your mouth." Water coursed over her body, and she pulled the curtain back all the way. "You see this?" She pointed to a hickey above her nipple. "I sure as hell didn't put this here. I'd say you're keeping up with me just fine."

"Oh, yeah?"

"Oh, hell no." She threw closed the shower curtain. "You are not coming in here. There is no way in hell your dick can even get up right now. It isn't scientifically possible."

"You wanna bet?" My dick was rock hard, and my hands were on my zipper.

"No, I do not want to bet because I'm pretty sure that is one bet I am going to lose because you are some sex freak that just can't seem to get enough of me. I really think we should consider getting you into some program to help curb your urges." She was babbling, and I was dropping my pants to the floor after I set the sodas on the counter.

She let out a startled scream when I pulled back the curtain, and she splayed her hands over her pussy and tits as if that was going to stop me from taking her against the shower wall. "Wrecker, my vajayjay can't handle much more."

"I'll take you from behind, babe."

Her jaw dropped, and she tilted her head to the side. "I don't think that's how it works."

I stepped into the tub and pulled her into my arms. "New angle."

"That's not how any of this works, Wrecker."

I turned her around in my arms and slid my hand down her slick body. "Bend over and I'll show you just how it works."

*

ALICE

He showed me just how it worked.
Lord. Have. Mercy.

*

CHAPTER 17

WRECKER

"What?"

"Wrecker, man. I need help."

I sat up and clutched the phone in my hand. "What the fuck is wrong?"

Boink was on the other end of the phone breathing heavily. "She's gone, man. They fucking took her."

"Raven?"

"Yes, Raven. She ended up being called into work tonight. I just pulled up to her apartment, and her door was wide open, and it looked like a damn tornado went through the place."

I threw back the covers and slipped out of bed without waking up Alice. After I had fucked her twice in the shower, we had eaten pizza, watched a couple of movies, and then passed out in bed. It had been a damn good night that was now being fucked up with the news Boink had just delivered to me. "Tell me everything you know." I closed the bedroom door behind me and stalked down the hallway.

"I just did, man. She worked. I kept an eye on her all night. No one talked to her besides the customers and one other waitress. She walked to her car. I gave her a five-minute head start because that's what I normally do. I walked to her front door, and the damn thing was wide open for anyone to walk in."

I laid my hand down on the counter and tried not to scream. "You didn't see anything on the drive to her place?" I really wanted to ask why in the fuck he gave her a five-minute lead, but that wasn't going to fix anything. Though yelling 'til I went hoarse was what I wanted, I kept a lid on it and tried to figure out what to do.

"Not anything out of the usual."

"Fuck."

"I'm sorry, brother. I was doing what you told me to do. I didn't want to get to close in case someone was watching her. I told you shit felt weird around there."

"Find the waitress she was talking to tonight."

"Mayra?"

"If that's her fucking name, then yeah. Find Mayra and see if she knows anything." The last time I had talked to Raven, which was before I had hooked up with Alice, she had talked about a waitress she had made friends with. I had to assume the Mayra he was talking about was the one she had been talking about.

"How am I supposed to find Raven?"

I rolled my eyes. "Well, since you couldn't seem to keep her safe, I'll be there to fucking find her." That was, if they hadn't done anything to her. I had to assume it was The Ultra who had nabbed her. "I'll be there by daylight."

"You want me to call the police to report her missing?"

"You don't even know her fucking last name, Boink. How the fuck are you going to report her missing? Tell them you had never talked to her, but you were watching her? They'd have you arrested within the hour. Find the other waitress. Talk to her. By the time you do that, I'll be in town." I jammed the end call button and tossed the phone on the counter.

Jesus Christ. I just couldn't catch a fucking break when it came to The Ultra. I combed my fingers through my beard and sighed. I was going to have to leave now, and I didn't know how long I was going to be gone. It was half-past three, and if I left now, I could be to Boink by six.

Unfortunately, The Ultra had tied my hands behind my back by grabbing Raven. I was going to have to show them all of my cards and pray they showed me some mercy. I just hoped Raven would be fine while I figured out how to get to Oakley.

Fifteen minutes later, I tossed Alice's helmet on the porch, threw my leg over the bike, and revved the engine. I had pressed a kiss to the side of her head, whispering to her that I needed to head out, and she had rolled over with a muttered grunt. The note I left on the counter was going to clue her in on where I was in the morning.

I hoped I wasn't going to be gone for a couple of days, but I really didn't have a clue what I was walking into.

I needed to get Raven out of whatever she was in and get back to Alice as soon as possible. Something with the way Boink talked told me that this wasn't going to be an easy fix. Then, I would be back in Kales Corners.

Fuck.

*

ALICE

Alice,
Got some shit to take care of.
I'll be gone for a bit.
Call me if you need anything.
- Wrecker

I flipped the paper over, hoping there was something more to the note than that, but it was blank.

I read it over two more times and finally set it down.

He was gone.

He was gone, and I had no freaking clue where the hell he was or when he would be back.

How the hell long was "for a bit?"

Two days? Four days? A month?

I mean, come on, throw a girl a bone here. I had spent days with the man, gotten used to him being around, and suddenly, he was gone without a reason. I'm sure it was club business, and I knew this is what Nikki and Karmen talked about when they said it drove them crazy when Nickel or Pipe would mumble about "club business" and they would just have to accept it.

I laid my palms on the counter and bit my lip. Well, now what was I supposed to do? Somehow, the man had come into my life like a freight train, and now, he was gone like a thief in the night. Though his note implied he would be back, but not when.

What was a girl to do when her bearded man went away indefinitely?

*

CHAPTER 18

WRECKER

"And why did you bring her here?"

Boink shoved his hands in his pockets. "She's scared, man. What the hell was I supposed to do? As soon as I mentioned that Raven was missing, she freaked the hell out."

"I don't know, but you didn't need to bring her here. Now we have another fucking chick we need to take care of. You assholes can't seem to do anything for me without tripping over some chick needing help."

Boink plopped down on the couch. "Hey, you're the one who's shacking up with his own chick that needs help."

"We aren't talking about me."

He raised his eyebrows. "Is that how that goes?"

I pointed toward the bedroom that Mayra was in. "I'm not taking care of whoever that is in the bedroom. You brought a chick into this that doesn't have jack shit to do with what is going on."

"She might have information about The Ultra. She has to know something that is going on since she about shit her pants and turned white as a damn ghost."

I ran my fingers through my hair. I had been in Riverton for four hours, and I hadn't figured a damn thing out about Raven. "Pump her for all the information you can, then get her the hell out of here."

"But what if she's in trouble with The Ultra now that she talked to us?"

I dropped my chin to my chest. Fucking hell. I didn't want this. I didn't fucking sign up for this shit when I got voted into being the president of the Fallen Lords. "I fucking hate all of you bastards. Herd these bitches like God damn cats into the clubhouse."

He held his hands up.

There was only one answer. "Find out what she knows, then take her back to the fucking clubhouse. Once we find out that The Ultra isn't on her case, we turn her loose. I've got too much fucking shit going on right now to deal with another chick."

"You won't even notice her."

That was a load of shit. I could only image the wagon-load of issues this chick had. "Load her up and get back to the clubhouse."

"You don't need me here?"

I leveled my gaze on him. "Because you did such a fucking good job of helping me already."

"I did everything you asked me to do, Wrecker. They made a move I didn't think that they would. How they figured out she was with the Lords is beyond me."

"Cause I'm sure you weren't as inconspicuous as you thought. Sitting on the same fucking barstool for three weeks and ordering the same thing puts you on their radar because even drunks aren't that routine." I'm sure he showed up as soon as Raven clocked in and then left as soon as she left. The club belonged to The Ultra, and I knew they kept tabs on everyone who came into that club. Up front was a bar and club, but behind the scenes, it was a hell of a lot more than that.

"What the hell was I supposed to do?"

"Something different that wouldn't have gotten Raven God damn kidnapped." I grabbed the keys to my bike and slid my sunglasses over my eyes. "Head back to Weston with Mayra. If I need any help, I'll let Pipe know." I couldn't blame this all on Boink, but he was the one available for me to yell at so he was going to get the brunt of my wrath.

I walked out of the hotel room without a backwards glance and jogged down the steps to my bike. I patted the pocket of my vest and pulled out a card I was hoping I wouldn't have to use. I had to basically promise my first born child and my Harley to get my hands on this number. After I got it, I was told to only use it if I was absolutely out of options.

Oakley Mykel
555- 617 - 8813

I was going to go directly to my problem now. Using Raven had backfired completely, and I had made a whole new mess to clean up.

There were two things I needed to do.

Get Raven out.

Get off The Ultra's radar.

*

CHAPTER 19

ALICE

"How long on that hash, Bos?"

"However long it takes."

I rolled my eyes and leaned against the back counter. It was Friday afternoon, and my shitty mood had worn off on Bos. We were both acting like bears with prickers in our paws. I missed Wrecker while I wasn't quite sure why Bos was being an ass more than usual. "Well, can you make that about thirty seconds? The customers actually want to eat today."

"Well, I want a vacation home in the Alps, but I'm still here cooking hash for you." He rattled the plate down on the pass-through and glared at me. "Hash, darlin'."

I grabbed the plate and set it on my tray along with the other three plates of food for the table. "I thought we were friends, Bos. Am I going to have to take you out for a drink tonight?"

"You feeling the need to get a little artistic on another ex-boyfriend's car?"

Now it was my turn to glare at him. "You've met all of my ex-boyfriends. You don't think he warranted me painting a pretty picture on his car?" I batted my eyelashes and popped the gum in my mouth.

"Not sure what exactly he did to you, but if he was as much of a pussy as he was that night, you should have drawn one of those vajayjays on his car."

My jaw dropped, and my gum tumbled onto the floor. "I don't think I ever thought I would hear that word come out of your mouth."

"You and Nikki used to say it all the time."

I tilted my head to the side. Nikki and I talked a lot when we were working, but I really doubt that every other word out of our mouths was vajayjay. "How about we just forget you ever said that and move on."

A huge grin spread across his lips. "Vajayjay."

A shiver coursed through my body. "Eww." I dropped down to pick up my gum and tossed it in the garbage. "We are not friends anymore." I grabbed the tray of food and balanced it on my shoulder.

"Oh no, I'll have to find another friend to take me out to bars and get arrested with."

I flipped him off and spun around. "I don't have to take this kind of abuse."

I delivered the food to the customers who were waiting and heard the bell above the door ding. "Grab a seat, I'll be right with you." I topped off table three's cups with soda, then pulled my notepad out of my apron as I walked to the customers who had just come in. "What can I get you fellas?"

Two handsome men with dark, tanned skin sat at the booth with no menus in front of them. They were dressed in nice suits that Kales Corners had never seen the likes of before. You could tell they were definitely just passing through.

"We'll just have coffee," the one on the left said.

"Uh, just coffee? We have some pretty good hash as long as Bos gets his ass moving and makes it," I talked loudly.

Bos grumbled from the kitchen, and a little smile crossed my lips. I loved giving that man hell.

"Coffee," the one on the right grunted.

I tucked my notepad back in my apron and gave them a tight smile. "Be right back, fellas." If all they wanted was damn coffee then they should have just stopped at the gas station right off the interstate.

"What do they want?" Bos grunted as I grabbed two cups and the coffee pot.

"Have no fear, nothing you need to do. They just want coffee."

"They here just for coffee?" he questioned.

He was just as suspicious as I was. "I know, right? They're going to be super disappointed when they taste the sludge I'm about to serve them."

Bos stepped to the side and looked at them over my shoulder. "Be careful around them, darlin'. They might be part of one of those sex rings."

"You mean trafficking rings, right? Cause a sex ring sounds like some people's personal kinks."

His gaze connected with mine. "You ever serious in your life, girl?"

I hooked the coffee cups though my thumb and shrugged. "If I was serious all the time, I would be crying constantly." I made my way back over to the table with the mysterious two men and set the cups down in front of them. "You two sure you don't want anything else to eat?"

The serious one who had grunted "coffee" at me shook his head. He held his phone up at me, the flash went off, and then he put it back in his pocket.

The other one tossed a twenty on the table, and they both stood up. "We're done here," somewhat nice guy said.

They walked out of the restaurant without a backward glance and got into a big black SUV.

"What in the hell was that?" Bos demanded.

I grabbed the empty cups and watched them back out of their parking spot and head in the direction of the interstate. "I ain't got no clue what the hell that was."

"Call your fella."

I turned to look at Bos. "My fella?"

"The guy with the massive beard. Call him and tell him what just happened."

"He's out of town, Bos."

"Don't fucking matter," he barked. "Call him, Alice. What just happened is not normal."

I haven't talked to Wrecker since he left three days ago. He had texted me twice, and I had replied each time, but he never texted me back right away. His note had said to call him if I needed anything, but I didn't want to bother him with something that might turn out to be nothing.

"Girl, I see your mind working all weird shit in your head right now. Call. Him. Now," Bos demanded.

I stuck my tongue out at him and set the coffee pot and cups down. "All right, all right. Don't get your Depends in a twist. It was probably nothing but a bunch of bored business dudes being assholes."

"Those were not the kind of businessmen you think they were, darlin'."

I rolled my eyes and pulled my phone out of my pocket. I fired off a quick text to Wrecker. **You busy?**

I waited a full ten seconds before he replied. **Not if you need me.**

Jesus. Talk about melting my heart in five words. **Something happened at the diner. Bos is freaking out and said I should call you. Can you talk?**

About to go into a meeting. Call right now.

I tapped on his name on the top of my screen and connected the call. "If I look like a fool, Bos, I'm kicking you in the nuts."

"Babe?" Wrecker said quietly.

Shit. "Uh, hi."

"Who you kicking in the nuts?"

I slid my finger across my neck and glared at Bos. He flipped me off and disappeared into the depths of the kitchen. "Bos. I might sound like a fool in ten seconds."

He chuckled low. "Tell me what's going on. I'm a few hours away, but if you need me, I'll have someone there quick."

My little heart fluttered at his words. *Focus, Alice.* "Um," I shook my head and gathered my thoughts. He had said that he was about to go into a meeting, so I needed to spit it out so he could get on with his shit. "About five minutes ago, two guys walked into the diner, sat down, and ordered coffee."

"Okay."

"When I brought them their cups, one of them pulled out their phone, took a picture of me, and then they left." The line was silent, but I could feel something change.

"What did they look like?" he growled.

"Uh, well. They had really nice suits on. Ones you wouldn't see in Kales Corners. Not like prom suites either, not polyester. More like Italia—"

"Alice," he snapped, cutting me off. "Their faces."

"Oh, um. They were really tan. Looked like they were maybe Italian. One was somewhat nice, and the other just sat there and said one word to me. Very rude, if you ask me."

"You get a look at their vehicle?"

Something wasn't right. He was much more concerned about this than I had thought he would be.

"Uh, big, black SUV. I think it was a Suburban. I know that because my mom used to have one. Not that nice, but you know what I mean."

"Which way did they head?"

"Toward the interstate."

"Is Bos still there?"

"Yeah, we're working, Wrecker."

He cleared his throat and lowered his voice. "I need you to do exactly what I say, Alice."

I nodded and realized he couldn't see me. "Okay," I replied.

"I'm going to call Brinks. He's going to come and get you. Stay with Bos until he gets there. Do not leave with anyone besides Bos and Brinks, you hear me?"

"Yes, Wrecker. But I don't—"

He cut me off. "I told you to just do what I say, Alice. I don't know what just happened, but I know that it's not good."

A chill ran down my spine. Wrecker sounded worried. I had never heard that tone from him before. "Wrecker, tell me what is going on."

"That's the thing, Alice. I don't have a fucking clue what is going on. Just do what I told you, and I promise you'll be safe."

I gulped and glanced back in the kitchen to see Bos watching me closely. "I'm scared, Wrecker," I whispered.

"Babe, I got you. Swear on my life, nothing will happen to you."

I closed my eyes and tried to get a grip on my anxiety that was going through the roof. "Stay with Bos, wait for Brinks. I can do that. What happens after Brinks gets here?"

"He'll take you back to the clubhouse. You'll be safer there than at your house. There are too many variables we can't keep you safe from there."

"Okay," I whispered. This was crazy. Wrecker was supposed to laugh at the guys and tell me to get back to work. Instead, he was freaking me the hell out. His tone was firm and unyielding. I wasn't going to argue with him about this. "So, Brinks will be here in two hours?"

"Probably quicker than that because I'm gonna tell him to break every damn speed limit to get you."

I dropped my chin to my chest and sighed. "Will I see you soon?" I wasn't going to calm down 'til I saw him again.

"Hopefully tonight, but I can't make any promises, babe. Just stay close to Brinks until I get back. I trust him with my life, and I know he won't let anything happen to you until I get there."

"Wrecker," I called. Hell, I was going to do it. I couldn't hang up with him without telling him what I was feeling.

"Yeah, babe?"

"I…I…fuck." The words were right there, but I was terrified to say them out loud.

"I hear you, babe. You don't need to say it out loud. I feel it."

He could feel that I loved him even though I couldn't get the damn words out. "Get back home to me."

"I'm always with you, babe, I'm always there." He disconnected the call, and I dropped the phone from my ear.

"What'd he say?"

I opened my eyes and saw Bos was standing right in front of me. "I have to stay with you until Brinks comes to get me."

"It's not good, is it?" he asked quietly.

I shook my head. "He didn't know what was going on, but I could tell that he was worried. He's sending Brinks, who he trusts with his life, to look after me until he gets home."

"When is that going to be?" he demanded.

"You sound like me, Bos. I just want him home, too, but he said he didn't know for sure."

Bos nodded. "Only saw the guy for about three minutes, darlin', but I knew that he was in love with you. He won't let anything happen to you."

My eyes bugged out, and my jaw dropped. I knew I loved Wrecker, but I guess my brain hadn't gotten that far into thinking that he loved me, too. "You don't know that, Bos. I don't know what I am to him, but I doubt that he loves me."

He rested his hand on my shoulder. "Don't ask me how I know, but I know it. Same way I knew that Pipe loved Nikki. These guys you ladies keep falling in love with may seem tough as nails, but I know when they do something, they don't half-ass it. If he's pulling every string possible to keep you safe, I know that he loves you. Don't doubt it, darlin'. Just accept it and know you won the damn lottery when it comes to men."

I swiped away a stray tear that streaked down my cheek. "I have never heard more sappier words in my life, Bos."

He took his hand off my shoulder and flipped me off. "Yeah, well, you ain't never gonna hear 'em again cause you gotta be damn sassy about it." He turned to walk back into the kitchen. "You got two hours 'til Brinks picks you up. Get these customers out of here, and we'll head back to your place."

"We don't close for another three hours, Bos."

He raised his hands in the air. "Don't care. Clear it out and lock the door. I'm not interested in more danger walking through that door." He disappeared through the swinging doors, and I looked at the two tables with customers in them.

They were all staring at me, and I realized they had heard every word Bos and I had said. "Uh, hey folks. As soon as you guys are done eating, I'm gonna ask you to leave."

They all instantly looked down at their plates then back up at me. "Or, I could get you all to-go containers."

A chorus of "to-go" went up. They weren't dumb. Even they knew two mysterious men walking into the diner were trouble.

I grabbed a handful of containers and passed them out to everyone. As soon as I handed them their checks, they all threw cash on the table and dashed out the door.

"Uh, mission accomplished," I hollered to Bos as I locked the door.

He walked out of the kitchen, and he turned out the back lights. "Figured they would get out of here fast. I called Mavis to let her know what was going on, and that I wouldn't be over tonight."

"What? Why?" I asked. "You just have to hang with me until Brinks gets here."

He shook his head. "Nope, I'm going with you, darlin'."

"Bos, that's crazy. There's no reason why you should."

"You and this Brinks guy are heading back to Weston on a motorcycle. Who's to say those goons in the Suburban aren't waiting for you as soon as you get on the interstate. I follow behind, and I can give anyone who follows you guys a little knock with the Buick."

"Bos, your car is like a tank. You give anyone a little knock with it, and they'll be in the ditch."

He shrugged and tossed me a damp rag. "If they're trying to hurt you, darlin', then that is where they belong." He pointed to the deserted tables. "Grab those dishes, toss 'em in the sink, and we're out." He left no room for argument.

After I cleared the tables, we argued about whether or not I should drive my car home.

"I hate you."

Bos backed out of his parking spot and headed to my house. My phone buzzed with a text message from a number I didn't know.

Be there in an hour. -Brinks

I quickly typed back where I was so he wouldn't go to the diner to get me.

Got it.

Brinks was apparently another one who used his words sparingly. "Must be a trait of the Fallen Lords," I mumbled. I tucked the phone in my purse and rested my head back against the headrest.

"All good?" Bos asked.

"Yeah. Brinks will be here in an hour." I closed my eyes and sighed.

After I got with Brinks, I was headed back to the clubhouse, but Wrecker still wasn't going to be with me. I wished there was something I could do to help him, but it seemed like I had just complicated things for him even more.

All I could do was comply with what he told me to do and wait.

I was never good at waiting.

*

Chapter 20

Wrecker

"Tell me, Wrecker. Just what is it you are doing here today?"

I sat back in my chair and crossed my arms over my chest. So, this was the game he was going to play. If he wanted to act like he didn't know about me, then I was going to inform him about who I was.

"I'm here because you seem to have something that belongs to me."

Oakley steepled his hands together and touched the tip of them to his lips. "Perhaps you'll have to be more specific than that. I always seem to have something that everyone always wants." He motioned around his office. "Fortune is high on the list of things that people covet from me."

I shook my head. "Your fortune is not one that I'm interested in." The Weston chapter of the Fallen Lords might not completely be on the up-and-up, but we were a hell of a lot cleaner than The Ultra. "I'm here about a girl that I think you might have acquired three days ago." After Boink had headed back to Weston with Mayra, I got in contact with Oakley. He put me off for three days before he agreed to meet with me last minute today.

"There are many women here, Mr. Wrecker. Many who choose to be here."

I leaned forward in my chair. "I'm interested in the ones who don't choose to be here."

A sly smile spread across his lips. "Then you are talking about only a handful. One being my sister, who I doubt you want. She's a mischievous thing of only twelve years who I unfortunately am her guardian." He leaned forward. "Unless you are in the market for something which I would be surprised you ask for."

With those words, I knew Oakley Mykel was the kind of evil most would never meet, and those who did never left his presence the same. "I'm not interested in your sister, and I hope she escapes your grasp."

He splayed he hands out in front of him. "My sister is of no concern to you from where I am sitting. From where I sit, I would say I have the upper hand, and you shouldn't be talking to me in a tone that one might take as hostile."

"I'm here for Raven." I was done beating around the bush. I could tell he was amused by it, and I didn't want to play into his pathetic game.

He leaned back in his chair. "Ah, yes. The feisty little one we brought in a few days ago."

"She belongs to the Fallen Lords."

"So she does." He tapped a finger to his chin. "So, one has to wonder why she was working in one of my clubs, asking questions that were bound to get her into trouble."

Just like Raven to not be patient and wait for things to happen. So, Boink hadn't done anything wrong, it was just Raven more than likely poking her nose into things that didn't have anything to do with her. "I had no idea she was here until one of her friends notified me that she had gone missing."

"But you knew what the club was about, didn't you?"

I nodded. I wasn't going to give him anything more than I needed to.

"You, of course, would know about the club and The Ultra since your fearless leader Jenkins has become an associate of mine."

I again nodded my head. I knew he wasn't a stupid man, just like he knew I wasn't either. His questions were a test, and I hoped my answers to would appease him.

"But why would you not share this information with your sister who somehow came to work for me?"

"My sister and I are not close."

"Then why do you care if she is under my roof?"

This is where I was going to have to tread lightly. "Though we may be distant, I wish no harm to come to her."

"So, you decided to come in here as the loyal older brother to save the day?"

"If she is here under her own accord, then you and I have nothing more to talk about when it comes to her."

He tilted his head to the side. "That sounds as if you have something else that we should talk about."

"We do have other business to discuss, but I would like to resolve the matter of my sister first."

Oakley snapped his fingers. "I have your sister, but first, I need you to stop lying to me, Mr. Wrecker." One of his men handed him a phone, then sank back into the corner where he was keeping watch. "I might have something on my phone that is of interest to you if you don't start talking to me straight."

I had been right. Oakley had sent his men to Alice. Though I didn't understand why they had only taken a picture and not her. They had already taken Raven, so what was one more woman to them?

"May I be frank with you, Mr. Mykel?"

He looked up from the phone and nodded. "To me, that is the only way to do business. Otherwise, misunderstandings start happening when someone does something they shouldn't."

I had no choice but to lay it out on the table for him to see. "I love my club, but the direction it is going as a whole is not one the Weston chapter wants to be a part of."

He nodded.

"Jenkins is working for you."

"I wouldn't go that far. He is an acquaintance that is providing me with a temporary service until I decide to terminate said service."

"Fair enough. The problem comes in where you being acquaintances with him puts me in a position to also be a part of that."

"Something you don't want to be a part of?" he asked.

"No, we don't see the need for us to go in the direction that Jenkins is headed."

He rested his hands on his desk. "You see, Mr. Wrecker, to me, this sounds like something you should be taking up with Jenkins, and not with me. Sending your sister into a place of business that I own did nothing more than poke a bear that did not need poking."

"I have tried numerous times to speak to Jenkins, but it falls on deaf ears. He has no wish to hear anything besides the sound of dollar signs."

"So, what would you like me to do about it? I'm a reasonable man when I'm not pushed into a corner and forced to take a woman to get someone's attention."

I held my hands up. "That is something I need to apologize for. Your reputation precedes you in the fact that you were not someone to negotiate with."

"But isn't that what we are doing right now? I repeat, I am a reasonable man when not fucked with."

"I would like to work out our own deal with you. One that only involves the Weston chapter of the Lords and will get me away from Jenkins."

He leaned back in his chair. "I'm listening."

I was going to give him the only thing I could. "You'll have the protection of the Lords, the Weston chapter. We've heard you are looking to branch out. Come further east."

"My production I have going right now is fine where it is. Though, you are correct in your knowledge of wanting to expand, but the expansion will be in the direction of guns."

I knew this. The intel Brinks had given me had been dead-on. "Guns fits much better in our wheelhouse than your other enterprises do." He had not yet said that they were heavy into running and cooking drugs, so I wasn't about to put that out there.

"What kind of protection can you offer me that I don't already have in my own men?"

I leaned forward. "My men are part of Weston." I tapped a finger onto his desk. "If you do this right, and come in quietly, you will get no resistance from the people of Weston. We can lay the groundwork allowing you to slide in without hassle."

"And in return, I give you back your sister and get Jenkins off your back."

I nodded.

"It seems as though you get two things, when I only get one. Not very fair, Mr. Wrecker."

I didn't have anything else to give him. Raven was of no use to him, so I didn't understand why he would want to keep her. "You only have to let Raven go and make one phone call to Jenkins to let him know the Weston chapter now works for you, under your command. For me to ease The Ultra into Weston, that is going to take months. You maybe have half an hour of work compared to me basically giving you my whole club until you get settled seems very fair in my book."

He tapped his finger on his chin. "I'm hearing what you are saying, but I don't like how you just come in here and get your way."

"I'm hardly getting my way. I'm giving you something to get back what you took from me."

He slammed his hand down on the table. "I took it from you because you stuck it under my nose. You were trying to get that woman into my inner sanctum, and that is something I do not appreciate at all. I like you more than that sniveling Jenkins, but the fact you thought you could pull one over on me infuriates me beyond reason."

I knew when I had sent Raven in that if she got caught, it was going to complicate things even more than they already were. "It was an error in judgement on my part. If I knew there had been another way at the time, I would have taken it instead."

Oakley closed his eyes and took a deep breath. "I'm going to take you up on your offer of expanding into Weston. I know from starting here in Riverton that being accepted by the community is hard especially when one comes in swinging their dick like they own the place." He shrugged. "We all learn as we go. Isn't that right, Mr. Wrecker? You've discovered that I'm actually a reasonable man, and I discovered that I would rather work with you than Jenkins."

"I feel like I need to repeat that we don't want anything to do with your business you already have running."

He held up his hands. "I hear you, I hear you. I won't force things on you that you don't want if I can take care of them in house, which is where that side of the business is going. I was soon going to alleviate Jenkins of his obligation to me, so it works in my favor that you are here ready to help me on my new venture."

I wasn't sure if I had done the right thing. If he was letting Jenkins out of his deal, that would have meant the Weston chapter would have been out of it too.

"I see where your thoughts are wandering, but I can assure that you making this deal with me works out much better for you. While I will be notifying Jenkins that I no longer need his service, that also means that chapter of the Lord's will no longer be in effect."

"You mean?"

Oakley drew a line across his neck. "It was an agreement that Jenkins and I made that when I no longer needed him, his club would no longer see the light of day. With you coming to me, it has granted that you will not be included in the termination of that chapter of the Lords."

"What about the two other chapters of the Lords?"

"Yours and Jenkins were the only ones we had spoken of when making our deal."

I growled at the knowledge Jenkins had bargained with my club without my knowledge. He may be the head of the club as a whole, but that didn't mean he could use us as he saw fit without input from all of us. "I'm not agreeing to those terms with our deal."

"I knew you wouldn't, seeing as you value human life much more than Jenkins did."

I couldn't say the same for him since he had been ready to offer his sister up to me ten minutes prior. Though with Oakley, that might have been a test to see just what kind of a person I was. "So, we are in agreement?"

"You help me set up shop in Weston, and I'll get Jenkins off your back."

"My sister," I growled.

He shrugged. "I'm still irritated by her ignorant attitude. You really need to get better people to be informants for you." He picked up his phone again and swiped to the right. "I'll give you back your sister, but you need to remember what kind of man I am, Mr. Wrecker." He held up his phone for me to see. Alice's surprised face stared back at me. She looked gorgeous but also confused as hell.

"So that means if I mess up, you'll mess with me."

He tucked the phone back into his pocket. "It means if you fuck with me, I'll rip your heart out by killing the woman you love."

*

224

Chapter 21

Alice

"Are you sure about this?"

Nikki set the bottle on the sink and nodded. "Yeah. I did this back in high school. It turned out amazing."

I closed my eyes and cringed. "Are you sure it's supposed to be stinging like this?"

She nodded again. "Yep, that means it's working."

I didn't know if it was working on burning all of my hair off or if the dye was working to make my hair dark purple. "Maybe I should have went to the salon."

"Nonsense," she muttered. "I got this from the store on Lofton. It was one of those beauty supply places. The chick behind the counter told me exactly how to do it. Two to one."

I opened one eye and looked up at her. "You said one to two when you were doing it before."

"That's not what I said," she insisted.

Oh, Jesus. All of this dye was either going to wash out, or it was going to give me third degree burns on my head. From the sting, I was leaning toward the third degree burns. "So how long does it sit on my head for?"

"Half an hour." She glanced at the clock that was behind me. "So, at twelve thirty, you'll be a purple bombshell." Nikki opened the fridge and offered me a wine cooler.

"You got anything stronger?" My nerves were already on edge with Wrecker still not back from wherever the hell he had went, and now, I had some purple goo on my head that may very well killing all of my hair as I sat there.

Nikki skipped out of the kitchen humming under her breath.

Yesterday, Brinks had picked me up and we had headed back to the clubhouse with Bos tailing behind us, ready to knock any bad guys who tried to mess with us off the road. He was disappointed when we had made it to the clubhouse without him having to give someone a little bump.

When we had walked into the clubhouse Nikki, Karmen, Cora, and Wren were all there. Apparently, Brinks had mentioned to Nickel that he was headed to pick me up so he had activated the Girl Gang phone tree to assemble everyone. Thankfully, they had told the girls enough to stop them from asking questions, but they were basically still clueless because none of the other girls were ever told everything that was going on.

They were all weirded out by the fact those guys took my picture and agreed it was best Wrecker had decided I should come to the clubhouse 'til shit got straightened out. So, last night, we had all got Girl Gang wasted and initiated Bos into the Girl Gang because I had told them how Bos had been there for me when I had drawn a dick on Mark Allen's car.

Surprisingly, Bos had fit right in with all of the girls. They sort of treated him like he was their dad, though Bos had decided to play pool all night with Brinks, Pipe, and Nickel.

Maniac had picked Wren up this morning to go get breakfast while Cora and Karmen were still in bed sleeping off last night's bender. Nikki had woken me up an hour ago to have coffee, and somehow, we had ended up in the kitchen with questionable purple dye on my head with Nikki running to go get some hair of the dog to combat the hangover we were both battling.

My phone buzzed in my pocket, and I picked it up to see Wrecker had texted me.

Be back to you tonight. Just a couple of things I need to do before I get to you.

I mass ya. Ugh. That's what I got when I typed too fast. **I miss you.** "There, much better," I mumbled.

Goof. He texted back.

I was never going to stop embarrassing myself in front of Wrecker. It was my destiny in life to be weird, crazy, and apparently, now a goof.

Ignore that first message.

No can do, babe. Gotta go. I'll see you tonight.

I shoved my phone back in my pocket and sighed. He was on the way home to me, but I wouldn't feel completely at ease until he was standing in front of me and I could pet his beard.

WRECKER

"This is the building that we have in mind for you guys." I pointed to a plot of land off the highway on the map. "It's still in the Weston township, but it's out of town a bit to where no one would be actively watching who was coming and going."

"But what about the police? It took me three years to get them used to my way of thinking here," Oakley questioned.

"The police won't be a problem as long you have the Lords behind you. You never noticed how we didn't get busted on any of those runs we went on for you?"

He nodded. "I didn't know if it was skill or luck. I'm assuming it was skill by the way you're not worried about the police."

"You're correct. The three deputies that patrol Weston are related to members of the club. As long as you guys don't go building your guns in the middle of the street in town, you won't have a problem from them."

Oakley sat back, pleased. "I have to say, Wrecker, you are much more organized than your counterpart in Riverton. I'm surprised you aren't the head of The Fallen Lords."

"Unfortunately, Jenkins was groomed by his father who was part of the original seven that formed the Fallen Lords."

"Ahh, family politics. Fucking over the hardworking ones who started from the bottom for years." He looked around his office. "That is why I started The Ultra. I worked for many men before I decided to go on my own. Each time, I got so close to being on the top only to be knocked down by a son, brother, or cousin that thought they had a right to my job just because of blood." He tapped his finger on the desk. "This was built off of sweat, not blood. Blood in my family is thinner than water."

"My sister is all that I have when it comes to family."

"But you have your woman," he pointed out.

"I do, as long you decide not to mess with her."

He held his hands up. "I feel much better about the agreement you and I have than the mess that Jenkins and I had going. Your woman is safe as long as you stick to our agreement. One, may I point out, that you brought to me."

He was right. This had all been my idea, but I knew the type of man Oakley was. If our deal became something he didn't like, he would manipulate it into something that he did like. "Nothing changes. You release Raven to me, get Jenkins off my back, and we help you."

"We've already shook on it, Wrecker. I may be a man that always tries to get what I want, but I do abide by deals. The reason I am terminating Jenkins is because he agreed to it. He was an idiot to agree to it, but he was so sure of the fact that he was indispensable." He leaned forward. "No one is that indispensable. One must learn how to move and grow. I think our agreement leaves room for both of those things to happen. Jenkins was stagnant. You and I will not be that."

I pushed the map toward him and stood up. "I think it's time for me to get out of here."

Oakley motioned to a guy to his right. "Bring Miss Raven up." The guy nodded and talked into a walkie-talkie attached to his shirt. "I hope she is returned to you acceptably. I was told that she was rather resistant when she was invited here."

I lifted an eyebrow. "Invited?" I chuckled.

He splayed his hands out. "We never intended to keep her. She was just a way that I was able to get your attention."

"You think you can keep your hands above the equator there, slimeball?"

"Ah, here is your charming sister now." Oakley stood up and nodded toward the back of the room.

"My brother is going to kick your ass when he finds out you guys took me." She was sassy as hell. Raven was the only chick I knew who would get kidnapped and three days later still be throwing sass around like it was confetti. Although, if it were Alice, she would be throwing jokes around like they were going out of style.

"He knows, Miss Raven."

Raven stopped trying to kick the guy who was holding her and looked up. "Well, what in the hell are you waiting for? Start kicking ass," she demanded.

I rolled my eyes and motioned to the guy to let her go. As soon as he released her arm, Raven threw an uppercut to his nose and stomped on his foot. "You take the guy behind the desk, I'll get the two by the door," she hollered.

I glanced over my shoulder to see Oakley shaking his head, and thankfully, he had a smile on his face. "Raven," I called. "Knock it the hell off before you get us killed."

She had her fist raised to clock the guy by the door in the head and turned her to look at me. "Uh, what?" she asked. "Why aren't you kicking ass?" She lowered her arm and frowned. "It's cause you're old, isn't it? Did you pull a hammy getting off of your bike to come rescue me?"

I looked back over at Oakley. "I can see why you guys grabbed her. I really didn't take into account the fact that Raven can't keep her mouth shut."

"Live and learn," Oakley replied quietly. "Now get her out of here before she hurts any more of my men. Milton's bleeding all over my new carpet thanks to her."

I grabbed Raven by the arm and pulled her out the door of Oakley's office.

"What are we doing?" she insisted as she struggled to get out of my hold. "We should be in there kicking their asses because they kidnapped me, Wrecker."

"They kidnapped you because you don't keep your mouth shut. I thought with age you would have figured that out, but obviously you haven't." One of Oakley's men guided us out of the house and over to my bike. I nodded to him, and he took a few steps back but didn't leave. Oakley and I might be in business together now, but he still didn't trust me.

The feeling was mutual.

"I'm only twenty-three, Wrecker."

I looked down at her. "And when I was twenty-three, I was the vice president of a motorcycle club. What the hell are you doing with your life besides getting covered in tattoos and getting kidnapped?"

"You told me to get intel," she spat. "How was I supposed to do that without asking questions?"

"Get on the bike," I barked. I wasn't going to go around with her about this right now.

"You better be taking me back to my house."

I shook my head. "No, your ass is coming back to the clubhouse. I think you need a little lesson on how to behave, Raven."

"You're not my father, Wrecker," she hissed.

"No shit, Raven."

She glared at me and crossed her arms over her chest. "I don't want to go back to your clubhouse."

"You don't have a choice." I pointed to the bike. "I'm getting on the bike and your ass better be planted on it two-point-five seconds after I sit down. Clear?"

She curled her lip and growled. "Yes, sir."

I threw my leg over the bike, sat down, and felt her move behind me. I slid my glasses over my eyes and started the bike. "I got a full tank of gas so we aren't stopping until we get to the club. Hold the fuck on."

She grabbed the bars under her seat and glared at me.

I kicked the bike up and drove down the winding driveway to the main road.

I had accomplished the two things I had set out to do. Though only one had gone the way I had planned. I had bound myself to The Ultra much more than I had hoped to. Brinks had given me the intel that Oakley was getting into guns, and I used it to our advantage. The club was going to have to understand that I didn't have much choice. That was the only way for me to get Raven back and to get out from under Jenkins.

Though I may have traded one evil for another kind.

Now, I had my bratty ass sister on the back of my bike and I was headed back to the club to tell them about the deal I had made and to finally see Alice.

It had been a long three days, and I missed her more than anything I ever had before.

*

CHAPTER 22

ALICE

"Oh, my God, it looks amazing."

I fluffed my hair and looked in the mirror again. "Really? Are you sure I don't look like Barney in drag?" My hair was purple. I'm talking purple with a capital P.

"It looks amazing, although I'm not sure why you are wearing a cow onesie when your man is on his way home after being gone for three days."

I looked down at my pajamas and laughed. "This was what Wrecker saw me in when he came over that night."

"Which night?" Karmen asked.

"The night of my mom's fun—" Fuuuuuck. That had come out of my mouth without even thinking about it.

Nikki and Karmen looked at each other and then at me. "Alice, what were you about to say?" Nikki asked.

"Um, my mom's fun night of fun." I cringed, praying to God they would buy what I had just said.

Karmen shifted Cole in her arms and leaned against the bathroom sink, blocking my view of the mirror. "Babe, did something happen to your mom? Is that why you went MIA for a while?"

I looked to the side and gulped. Did I really need to keep this secret from them anymore? I wasn't okay with my mom being gone, but it had gotten easier remembering her and not being sad too much. "Uh, my mom passed away a little bit ago."

"Oh, my God," Nikki gasped. "Why in the world didn't you tell us? We would have been there in a heartbeat." She wrapped her arms around me and laid her head on my shoulder.

I felt the tears coming, but I didn't want to give into them. "I...just...I didn't know how to say it."

"You say it by calling us up and telling us to get our asses there now." Karmen joined in on the hug and put the arm that wasn't holding Cole around Nikki and me. "You must have went through hell all by yourself," she mused.

"Um, Wrecker was there right after the funeral," I confessed.

Nikki raised her head and looked offended. "He knew and he didn't tell us," she exclaimed.

"Don't be mad at him," I said quickly. "I told him not to tell anyone. I didn't want to bother you guys with it."

"Jesus Christ," Karmen whispered. "Girl, do we need to go over the rules of the Girl Gang? I thought you of all people would know how to activate the stress call."

"We have a stress call?" Nikki asked.

"I think you guys mean a distress call."

Karmen shook her head. "No, that means you're fine. Stress call means you're in stress." She tilted her head to the side. "At least, that's what I think." She swatted her hand. "Oh, who the hell knows. You should have put up the Girl Gang signal and we would have come running."

"Is that like the bat signal, because I am down for getting a big ol' light and shining it into your guys' windows when I need you." I was so going to piss off Nickel and Pipe with that thing if we decided to get one. "Can it be in the shape of a penis?"

Karmen snapped her fingers in my face. "Woman, focus. We're trying to comfort you about your mom."

I grabbed her hand. "I'm okay, Karmen." And I was. It still hurt, but I knew that I was going to be okay. "I didn't know how to deal with it, but Wrecker helped me."

"Well, what in the hell did he do?" Nikki demanded.

My head tipped to the side, and I smiled. "He didn't do anything," I laughed. "Well, he let me be me. That's all he did."

"Well, hell, we let you be you, too," Karmen insisted.

Nikki elbowed her in the side. "It's not the same, dumb-dumb."

"Well, it should be. We've known you longer than he has."

"Yeah, but I see her a hell of a lot better than you two do."

Karmen and Nikki both jumped and spun around. "My God!" Nikki screeched.

"Just call me Wrecker, darlin'."

Nikki flipped him off.

"You could have given me a heart attack. I'm holding Cole, and I might have dropped him if my heart went down!" Karmen scolded him.

Wrecker held his hands up. "My apologies, ladies. I just heard Alice was in my room and I came to find her."

"Well, next time, knock over a lamp or something." Nikki clutched a hand to her chest and sighed. "You should really put a bell on your vest. You're way to stealthy." She looked over her shoulder at me. "We'll leave you to your man, but you better believe we're not done yelling at you for not telling us everything that is going on in your life."

"Is that part of the Girl Gang code?" I quipped.

Karmen pointed at me. "It sure the hell is." She glared at Wrecker as she ducked past him. "Could you seriously not have such big shoulders. I mean really," she mumbled. She turned sideways to make it out of the doorway and still bumped against him.

Nikki patted him on the shoulder. "I think you can skip a couple of days in the gym there, big guy."

Wrecker turned to the side and let her pass easier than he had Karmen.

"Your chicks are just as crazy as you are." He stepped into his room and shut the door behind him. I was still standing in the bathroom, but I was now grasping the sink. He was back, and he was in one piece. I didn't realize how much I had missed him 'til he had texted me to say he was on the way home.

"Uh, yeah." Crazies stuck together. And then they made up a Girl Gang.

"You gonna stay over there, or am I going to have to come and get you?"

"You might have to come and get me. Some weird shit is going on right now."

"Weird shit?" He quirked an eyebrow, and I swear to Christ, my panties went up in flames.

"Stop that," I scolded. "Can you not see I can barely stand? You do that thing with your eye, and I'm ready to melt into a puddle on the floor."

"My girl missed me," he muttered.

"If you could sound less smug about that, I would appreciate it. I can't even crack a joke right now because you've completely scrambled my brain. I don't know whether to jump your bones or tell you that I love you." I slapped a hand over my mouth and wheezed.

"That sounded even better than I imagined it would."

I closed my eyes and turned to face the mirror. "Would you just shut up, Alice?" I whispered.

"Are you talking to yourself, babe?"

I glanced over to see him bent over, untying his boots. "Yes. You're interrupting."

"Why don't you talk to me?" He stood up and kicked off his boots. He pulled his shirt over his head and tossed it on the floor. "I'm always willing to listen, babe."

"You know how Nikki said you could skip a couple of days at the gym?" He nodded. "Don't listen to a word she said. I fully appreciate the time you put in and would like to touch your hard-earned muscles. All over."

He held his arms out wide. "I'm all yours, babe. Just get your ass over here."

I let go of the sink, sprinted from the bathroom, and launched myself into his arms. "That was an offer I couldn't refuse." His arms wrapped tight around me, and his lips claimed mine.

I could kiss Wrecker forever and never get enough of him. His lips were soft and tender yet they demanded more and more from me with each kiss. "Bed," I whispered against his lips.

He took three large steps backward and fell onto the bed with me on top of him. "How much did you miss me?"

I reached up and stroked his beard. "You were gone?" I teased.

He slapped my ass and growled deep. "Maybe you missed my beard and not me."

"Hmm, that might not be entirely true. There are other things about you that I missed." I ran my hand down his chest and rested it against his tattooed skin.

"And what would those things be?"

"I'm kind of a fan of your shoulders. Your chest ah-mazing, and well," my eyes darted down between us, "your Mega Weiner."

He chuckled, and his body rumbled underneath me. "I've never laughed so much in my life before you, babe."

I shrugged one shoulder. "It's a skill."

He brushed my hair out of my face and tucked it behind my ear. "Rewind to when you said you loved me. I need to hear it again."

Yeah, that was going to be a no. "I think you're hearing things, Wrecker. You should totally get that checked out."

"Is that how it's going to be?" His hands moved to my ribs. "Admit you love me, or you're going to endure my wrath."

I rolled my eyes. "Pfft, what are you going to do? Tick—"

His fingers lightly moved over my sides, and I couldn't help the laughter that bubbled from my lips. "That's not fair," I squealed. He was tickling the hell out of me, and I couldn't get away from him. I rolled off to the side, and he followed me. He tangled his legs with mine and held me in place with his weight. "You can't do this to me," I wheezed.

"Admit you love me," he insisted.

"Goonies never surrender," I laughed.

"You're hardly a goonie, babe," he chuckled.

"Stop, stop," I pleaded.

His hands stopped moving, but he didn't move them away from my sides. "Do you have something else to say?"

"I love your beard," I admitted.

He quirked an eyebrow.

I closed my eyes and shook my head. "Would you stop doing that?"

"Doing what?"

"That eye thing, and, well, just breathing in general because no matter what you do, it drives me crazy," I mumbled.

I felt his breath against the skin of my neck. "Tell me what you said before, Alice, and I promise to go gentle on you," he whispered in my ear.

"What if I don't want gentle?" Jesus. I really needed to learn how to vet my thoughts before I said them out loud.

He nipped at my ear. "I'll give it to you however you want, babe."

A full-on shiver coursed through my body. "And all I need to do is say three little words?" They were just words, after all. Words that meant a shit-ton, but I meant them. Even though I was terrified to say them out loud again. "Can we say them together? On the count of three?"

Wrecker rolled his eyes, but he nodded. "One, two, three." I took a deep breath and closed my eyes. "I love you." My eyes snapped open and looked up at the handsome devil who hadn't opened his mouth after I said three. "You're an ass!"

He pressed his lips against mine, and I felt his lips curve into a smile while he kissed me. "Yeah, but you love me," he mumbled.

"Take backs," I exclaimed.

He grabbed my wrists and held them over my head. "No."

"Yes," I insisted.

"You can't take it back because I love you, too."

My breath whooshed out of my lungs, and my world came to a screeching halt. "You love me," I whispered.

"It was kind of inevitable after I saw you in this sexy cow onesie."

I batted my eyelashes. "The boys always go crazy over it."

"I can only imagine," he laughed.

"So, what do we do now that we love each other?" I asked.

He reached for the full body zipper of my pajamas and slowly unzipped 'til my breasts were uncovered. "Babe, you're naked under here."

"Uh, duh. These fuckers get hot." Had he never worn a onesie before? I mean damn, they were made out of fucking fleece sometimes. "If I wore clothes under this thing, it would smell like two rats fucking in a burlap sack when I took it off." He opened his mouth, and I pressed a finger to his lips, silencing him. "Don't ask how I know what that smells like."

He nipped at my finger and rolled us over again so I was lying on top of him. "I really need to learn how to go with whatever comes out of your mouth, don't I?"

"It would save a lot of confusion and talking."

"Silence," he whispered.

"It would definitely leave a lot of room for silence," I agreed.

"Then shut up and let me fuck you, babe."

Who was I to argue with him? Silence was becoming my new favorite thing.

*

CHAPTER 23

WRECKER

"You don't think you should have mentioned that your sister was here?"

I shrugged and pulled my shirt over my head. "Had other shit on my mind than my bratty little sister."

She laid a hand on my chest and looked up at me. "You mean to tell me that the male equivalent of you is in the clubhouse? How can anything be more important than that?"

"Telling you I loved you seemed just a bit more important."

She slugged my shoulder. "After you made me say it."

I grabbed her hand and pressed a kiss to her knuckles. "You can meet her now, babe. I'm warning you, though. She's kind of a bitch."

"Wrecker," she gasped. "How can you say that about your sister?"

"You don't have any brothers or sisters, do you, babe?"

She shook her head.

"Then you wouldn't understand how I could say something like that. My mom had her when I was ten, and by the time she was five, she ruled the house. I left when I was eighteen 'cause I couldn't put up with that shit."

"But what happened when your parents passed away?"

I ran my fingers through my hair. "I tried to get custody of her, but I couldn't. She was seventeen and got put into foster care for a year. I tried to stay in touch with her during that time, but she was just pissed off at the world."

Alice frowned and laid her hand on my chest. "That must have been really hard for her, Wrecker."

"It was, babe. There wasn't anything I could have done about it, though. I was the president of an MC and didn't have a physical address. There wasn't a court around that would give me custody of a seventeen-year-old."

"And now, she hates you."

I tucked her hair behind her ear. "I think saying Raven hates the world is a better statement."

Alice cringed. "Lordy."

Yeah. Shit with Raven wasn't good. If I was honest with myself, I should have tried a hell of a lot harder to get custody of her, but I hadn't. "Just try not to take what she says to heart. She tends to say the truth even if she shouldn't."

"Um, I hate to break it to you, Wrecker, but you are the same way."

I shook my head. "My delivery is a hell of a lot better than hers."

Alice rolled her eyes and threaded her fingers through mine. "I think you might be delusional,

Beardilocks." She pulled me out of my room and down the hallway to the common room. "I need to meet her."

"She doesn't have a beard," I whispered loudly.

The glare she gave me over her shoulder could have frozen half of Weston. "Do not repeat what I said to you before. I was probably drunk."

She had been, but that didn't mean I was going to forget what she had said.

"Who the hell is that?" Alice squawked. "There are two chicks I've never seen before."

Raven and Mayra were sitting on the couch talking to Cora. "Fuck. I forgot about Mayra."

"Mayra?" Alice looked up at me. "Are you recruiting chicks for the Girl Gang now?"

"No," I growled. "You and your chicks are not bringing her into whatever gang it is you guys think you have. She is only here for the night and then she is heading back to wherever the hell it was Boink got her from."

"Wrong," Raven called. "As long as you make me stay here, Mayra stays too."

"How did she hear you?" Alice whispered. "Does she have bionic hearing?"

"Negative, babe. She just can't seem to keep her nose out of shit that doesn't have anything to do with her."

Alice looked at Raven who had turned on the couch and was now glaring at me. "Does your chick have a name, or are you just showing her the door?"

Alice gasped, and I flexed my fist.

"Girl, I like you, but you might want to check that attitude just a bit." Cora stood up and shook her head. "I don't like being here, but I don't take it out on the ol' ladies. Check yourself before you wreck yourself."

Raven glared at Cora. "Last I checked, I didn't ask for your help on fitting in around here."

Cora pointed at me. "Good luck with that one. I feel sorry for the fool who falls in love with her."

Now, if that wasn't the damn truth. Whoever tried to tangle with Raven was going to have to be able to go twelve rounds. "You wanna say hi to Alice before you insult her anymore?"

"I still like you, girlie, but you're going to have to learn your place here," Cora said to Raven. She winked at Alice then walked out the front door.

"I never thought the day would come that I would say I like Cora better than someone else," I muttered.

Alice grabbed onto my arm and pulled me toward Raven. "Just introduce me. She's not that bad."

Alice had no idea the bite Raven had behind her bark. "Put the claws in for two minutes, Raven," I warned.

She glared at me and crossed her arms over her chest.

"Hey, I'm Alice."

Raven looked her up and down, and I was thankful that Alice had put on jeans and shirt instead of the onesie she had on before. "Your shirt is dumb."

Alice looked down and laughed. She was wearing shirt that said "Team awkward here to make things weird." It was different, but it was totally Alice. "Thanks."

Raven tilted her head to the side. "Who did your hair?"

She ran her fingers through her hair. "Nikki and Karmen. It's pretty funky, right?"

I had noticed she had dyed her hair, but I hadn't said anything because I was too concerned with getting her clothes off before. "I like it."

Alice looked up at me and beamed. "Thanks, Mr. President."

Raven made a gagging sound and stuck her finger in her mouth. "Maybe you two should head back to your room."

Alice turned to Mayra. "Hey, you must be Mayra."

Mayra meekly waved. "Hey."

This chick screamed issues. I had only met her for two minutes before Boink had convinced me she needed to come back to the clubhouse. When I spent time with Oakley, I had discussed her with him. He hadn't even known her name and had to ask one of his guys who she was. She wasn't on anyone's radar and didn't need to be at the clubhouse. Raven, on the other hand, needed to be here. She had pissed off Oakley, and while he said that he was over it, I didn't want to risk Raven doing something dumb and fucking up the deal I had struck with him. Except now, it seemed the only way I was going to be able to keep her here was if Mayra stayed with her. How these two had become friends was beyond me.

"Are you guys doing okay? Are your rooms good?"

"We're sharing a room," Raven replied, her tone bored.

Alice leaned closer to Mayra. "I would totally demand bunk beds if I were you."

A light laugh drifted from Mayra's lips, and Raven just glared at Alice.

Raven was definitely going to be a work in progress. She had a chip on her shoulder the size of Texas, and it was going to take a fuck lot to knock it off. Raven jumped off the couch and called for Mayra to follow her.

"It was nice meeting you," Alice sang out.

Mayra waved, a hesitant smile on her lips, and Raven flipped us off behind her back.

Alice dissolved into a laughing mess as soon as they were out of earshot. She held onto my shoulders and tried not to fall over. "Your…sister is…such a…bitch." She peeled off into a spurt of laughter.

"I'm glad you find this so funny. I was afraid she was going to send you running for the hills."

Alice shook her head and wiped the tear that had streaked down her cheek from laughing so hard. "I like her, but damn, Wrecker, you are going to have your hands full with her. I don't even think the Girl Gang is going to be able to snap her out of whatever is going on in her head."

"I don't even know what is going on in her head."

Alice sobered and rested her head on my shoulder. "I did like all of her tattoos, though. That seems to be the one thing you guys have in common."

"That is the only thing, babe."

She sighed and pressed a kiss to my lips. "You'll figure her out, Wrecker. Who knows, maybe one of the guys will take a shine to her and they can work out all of her problems."

"I wouldn't wish her on any of the guys, babe." My sister was a fucking mess who was going to take a hell of a lot more than some guy coming into her life.

Alice wrapped her arms around my neck and pulled me close. "Don't worry, Mr. President. You don't have to solve all the club's problems in one day."

"That's my job, though, babe."

She pressed another kiss to my lips. "How about for the rest of the day, the only thing you have to deal with is silence?" She wiggled her eyebrows and bumped her chest against me.

I stroked my beard. "Silence, huh?"

She nodded and turned her head. She pressed a kiss to my ear and whispered, "But first, you're going to have to catch me." She took off down the hallway and threw a sexy wink at me over her shoulder.

Silence was the thing that was going to make up for the attitude Raven had just thrown at me. I would deal with her another day. Hell, it was going to take a hell of a lot longer than a day to deal with her.

Right now, all I wanted was to lock Alice in my room and not come out until morning.

"Oh, Mr. President," she called. The black shirt she had been wearing came sailing down the hallway and landed in front of my feet.

"Woman, you better not be in that hallway with no shirt on," I called. I grabbed her shirt and strutted down the hallway. I saw her purple hair flying right before she turned the corner down to our room.

She was so going to get it.

*

CHAPTER 24

ALICE

"I had a damn tank top on," I grumbled.

"How in the hell was I supposed to know that?"

I rolled over on my side and pointed to my butt. "I don't know, but my ass is totally going to have a handprint on it come morning."

He glided a hand over my soft skin and squeezed gently. "I didn't spank you that hard."

"Yeah, and I didn't draw a dick on Mark Allen's car." I rolled my eyes and eased back over to my stomach.

Wrecker draped his body over me and pressed a kiss to my neck. "You ever going to tell me what happened with him?"

"Not a snowball's chance in Hell."

"Really?" he grumbled.

That was one story I was going to take to the grave with me. Or until I got rip-roaring drunk and forgot that I never wanted to tell anyone that story. "Really."

He lightly spanked my ass again. "I'll get it out of you one day. I'm sure, in regular Alice style, it's gonna be a crazy story."

I rolled my eyes. "My lips are sealed." Going to the grave with that one.

"Babe," he growled.

I glanced over my shoulder at him and smiled. "For once, that one word is not going to work on me. Maybe one day, you'll find out the story, but today is not that day."

"It's a damn good thing I love you," he mumbled. He pressed wet, hot kisses to my shoulder and brushed my hair to the side. "Otherwise, I'd have a talk with Mike Billy to find out just what happened."

Ha. He wouldn't find anything out that way either, but I would let him think that if he really wanted to, he could figure out what happened. "But you do love me and you'd never do that."

"That I do, babe."

I sighed and laid my head down. "Wrecker loves Alice," I sang out.

"And Alice loves Wrecker," he chimed in.

I did. Through everything that had happened to me in the past month, I had managed to come out on the other end different, but still happy.

Wrecker loved me, and with him next to me, I would never be alone.

*

CHAPTER 25

MAYRA

I was safe here.

Nobody could find me here.

I glanced over at Raven, who was fast asleep, and tugged my pillow case off. I pulled the small envelope out and patted it gently.

Even if they found me, as long as I had this envelope, they could never touch me.

THE END

About The Author

Winter Travers is a devoted wife, mother, and aunt turned author who was born and raised in Wisconsin. After a brief stint in South Carolina following her heart to chase the man who is now her hubby, they retreated back up North to the changing seasons, and to the place they now call home.

Winter spends her days writing happily ever after's, and her nights zipping around on her forklift at work. She also has an addiction to anything MC related, her dog Thunder, and Mexican food! (Tamales!)

Winter loves to stay connected with her readers. Don't hesitate to reach out and contact her.

http://www.facebook.com/wintertravers

Twitter: @WinterTravers

Instagram: @WinterTravers

http://www.wintertravers.com/

Coming Soon

Holeshot
Nitro Crew Series
Book 2
September 29th

LOVING LO
DEVIL'S KNIGHTS SERIES
BOOK 1

WINTER TRAVERS

Chapter 1
Meg

How did just stopping quickly to get dog food and shampoo turn into an overflowing basket and a surplus pack of paper towels?

"Put the paper towels down and back away slowly," I mumbled to myself as I walked past a display of air fresheners and wondered if I needed any.

"Oh dear. Oh, my. I... Ah... Oh, my."

I tore my thoughts away from air fresheners and looked down the aisle to an elderly woman who was leaning against the shelf, fanning herself. "Are you ok, ma'am?"

"Oh dear. I just... I just got a little... dizzy." I looked at the woman and saw her hands shaking as she brushed her white hair out of her face. The woman had on denim capris and a white button down short sleeve shirt and surprisingly three-inch wedge heels.

"Ok, well, why don't we try to find you a place to sit down until you get your bearings?" I shifted the basket and paper towels under one arm to help her to the bench that I had seen by the shoe rack two aisles over. "Are you here with anyone?" I asked, as I guided her down the aisle.

"Oh no. I'm here by myself. I just needed a few things."

"I only needed two things, and now my basket is overflowing, and I still haven't gotten the things I came in for."

The woman plopped down on the bench chuckling, shaking her head. "Tell me about it. Happens to me every time too."

"Is there something I can do for you? Has this happened to you before?" She was looking rather pale.

"Unfortunately, yes. I ran out of the house today without eating breakfast. I'm diabetic. I should know by now that I can't do that." My mom was also diabetic, so I knew exactly what the woman was talking about. Luckily, I also knew what to do to help.

"Just sit right here, and I'll be right back. Is there someone you want to call to give you a ride home? Driving right now probably isn't the best idea." I set the basket and towels on the floor, keeping my wallet in my hand.

"I suppose I should call my son. He should be able to give me a ride," the woman said as she dug her phone out of her purse.

I left the woman to her phone call and headed to the candy aisle that I had been trying to ignore. I grabbed a bag of licorice, chips, and a diet soda and went to the checkout. The dollar store didn't offer a healthy selection, but this would do in a pinch. The woman just needed to get her blood sugars back up.

I grabbed my things after paying and headed back to the bench. I ripped open the bag and handed it to the woman. "Oh dear, you didn't have to buy that. I could have given you money."

"Don't worry about it. I hope if this happened to my mom there would be someone to help her if I wasn't around."

"Well, that's awfully sweet of you. My names Ethel Birch by the way."

"It's nice to meet you, Ethel. I'm Meg Grain. I also got you some chips and soda." I popped opened the soda and handed it to Ethel.

"Oh, thank you, honey. My son is on the way here, should be only five minutes. You can get going if you want to, you don't need to sit with an old woman," Ethel said as she ate a piece of candy and took a slug of soda.

"No problem. The only plans I had today was to take a nap before work tonight. Delaying my plans by ten minutes won't be a problem."

"Well, in that case, you can help me eat this licorice. It's my favorite, but I shouldn't eat this all by myself. Where do you work at?" Ethel asked as she offered the bag to me.

"The factory right outside of town. I work in the warehouse, second shift." I grabbed a piece and sat down on the floor. If I was going to wait for Ethel's son to show up, might as well be comfortable while I waited for him.

"Really? Never would have thought that. Figured you would have said a nurse or something like that. Seems like you would have to be tough to work in a warehouse, sounds like a man's job."

I laughed. "Honestly, Ethel that is not the first time I have heard that, and it probably won't be the last. You need a certain attitude to deal with those truckers walking through the door. I have an awesome co-worker, so he helps out when truckers have a problem with a woman loading their truck."

"Sounds like you give them hell. My Tim was a trucker before he passed. I know exactly what you are talking about." Ethel took another drink of her soda and set it on the bench next to her.

"Feeling better?"

"Surprisingly, yes. It's a wonder what a little candy can do. How much do I owe you?" Ethel asked as she reached for her purse by her feet.

"Don't worry about it. I'm just glad that I was here to help."

"Mom! Where are you?" Someone yelled from the front of the store.

"Oh good, Lo's here. You'll have to meet him." Ethel cupped her hands around her mouth and yelled to him she was in the back.

I started getting up off the floor and remembered I wasn't exactly as flexible as I use to be while struggling to get up.

"Ma, you ok?" I was halfway to standing with my butt in the air when his voice made me pause.

It sounded like the man was gurgling broken glass when he spoke. Raspy and *so* sexy. Those three words he spoke sent shocks to my core. Lord knows the last time I felt anything in my core.

"Yes, I'm fine. I forgot to eat breakfast this morning and started to get dizzy when Meg here was nice enough to help me out until you could get here." Ethel turned to me. "Lo, this is Meg, Meg this is Lo."

Oh, lord.

I couldn't talk. The man standing in front of me was... oh, lord. I couldn't even think of a word to describe him.

I looked him up and down, and I'm sure my mouth was hanging wide open. I took in his scuffed up motorcycle boots and faded, stained ripped jeans that hugged his thighs and made me want to ask the man to spin so I could see what those jeans were doing for his ass. I moved my eyes up to his t-shirt that was tight around his shoulders and chest and showed he worked out.

I couldn't remember the last time I worked out. Did walking to the mailbox count as exercise? Of course, I only remembered to get the mail about twice a week, so that probably didn't count.

His arms were covered in tattoos. I could see them peeking out from the collar of his shirt and could only imagine what he looked like with his shirt off. Tattoos were my ultimate addiction on a man. Even one tattoo added at least 10 points to a man's hotness. This guy was off the fucking charts.

My eyes locked with his after my fantastic voyage up his body, and I stopped breathing.

"Hey, Meg. See something you like, darlin'?" Lo rumbled at me with a smirk on his face.

Busted. I sucked air back into my lungs and tried to remember how to breathe.

Lo's eyes were the color of fresh cut grass, bright green. His hair was jet black and cut close to his head with a pair of kick ass aviators sitting on top of his head. He was golden tan and gorgeous. The man was sex on a stick. Plain and simple.

"Uh, hey," I choked out.

Lo's lips curved up into a grin, and I looked down to see if my panties fell off. The man had a panty-dropping smile, and he wasn't even smiling that big. I would have to take cover or risk fainting if he smiled any bigger.

"Thanks for looking after my ma for me. I'm glad I was in town today and not out on a run," Lo said.

Ok. Get it together Meg. You are a 36-year-old woman, and this man has rendered you speechless like a sixteen-year-old girl. I needed to say something.

"Say something," I blurted out. Good Lord did I just say that. Lo quirked his eyebrow, and his smirk returned.

"Ugh, I mean no problem. I didn't do that much. No problem." I looked at Ethel while Lo was smirking at me; Ethel had a full-blown smile on her face and was beaming at me.

"You were a life saver, Meg! I don't know what I would have done if you weren't here." Ethel looked at Lo and grinned even bigger.

"You should have seen her, Lo. She knew just what to do to help me. I could have sworn she was a nurse the way she took charge. She's not, though, just has a good head on her shoulders and decided to help this old lady out."

"That's good, Ma. You got all your shit you need so we can get going? I got some stuff going on at the garage that I dropped to get over here fast."

I took that as my cue to leave and ripped my eyes off Lo and bent over to get my basket and paper towels.

"Yes son, that's my stuff right here. I just want to get Meg's number before she leaves."

"Why do you need my number?" I asked, as I juggled my basket and towels.

Ethel grabbed her purse off the ground and started digging through it again. "Well, you won't let me pay you back for the snacks you got for me so I figured I could pay you back by inviting you over for dinner sometime. So, what's your number, sweetheart?"

"I don't eat dinner," I blurted out. I was going to have to have a talk with my brain and mouth when I got home. They needed to get their shit together and start working in unison so I wouldn't sound like such an idiot.

"You don't eat dinner? Please don't tell me you're on a diet." Lo said as he looked me up and down.

"No," I said. Lord knew I should be.

Lo and Ethel just stared at me.

"So, no, you don't eat dinner?" Lo asked again.

"Yes. I mean no, I'm not on a diet. Yes, I eat dinner. I just work at night, so I meant that I wouldn't be able to come to dinner." I looked at Lo and blushed about ten shades of red. "Why is this so hard?"

"What's hard, sweetheart? Can't remember your phone number? I can barely remember mine too. Don't worry about not being able to make it to dinner; I can have you over for lunch. You eat lunch right?" Ethel asked with a smirk on her face. Lo had a full-blown smile on his face, even his eyes were smiling at me. That smile ought to be illegal.

I could see where Lo got his looks from. With Lo and Ethel standing next to each other, I could totally see the resemblance. Especially when they were both smirking.

I had to get out of here. I'm normally the one with the one-liners and making everyone laugh, now I couldn't even put two words together.

"Lunch would be good." I rattled off my number, and Ethel jotted it down.

"Ok, sweetheart, I'll let you get your nap. I'll give you a call later, and we can figure out a day we can get together." Ethel shoved the pen and paper back in her bag and leaned into me for a hug.

I awkwardly hugged her back and patted her on the shoulder. "Sounds good. Have a good day, Ethel. Uh, it was nice meeting you, Lo," I mumbled, as my gaze wandered over Lo again.

"You too Meg. See you around," Lo replied.

I gave them both a jaunty wave and booked it to the checkout. Thankfully there wasn't a line, and I quickly made my escape to my car. I threw my things in the trunk and hopped in. I grabbed my phone out of my pocket and plugged it into the radio and turned on my chill playlist, as the soothing sounds of Fleetwood Mac filled the car.

Music was the one thing in my life that had gotten me through so much shit. Good or bad, there was always a song that I could play, and it would make everything better. Right now, I just needed to unscramble my brain and get my bearings. Fleetwood Mac singing "Landslide" was helping.

I pulled out of the parking lot and headed home. All I needed was to forget about today. If Ethel called for lunch, I would say yes because she did remind me so much of mom, but I wasn't going to let Lo enter my thoughts anymore. A woman like me did not register on his radar, he was better just forgotten.

When I was halfway home, I realized I forgot dog food and shampoo.

Shit.

Lo

I helped mom finish her shopping and loaded all her crap into the truck. I looked around the parking lot for Meg, hoping she hadn't left yet so I could get another look at her. As soon as I saw her ass waving in the air as she struggled to stand up, I knew I had to be inside her.

It took all my willpower to not get a hard-on as her eyes ran over my body. Fucking chick was smoking' hot and didn't even know it.

"Thanks for coming to get me, Lo," Ma said as she interrupted my thoughts about Meg.

"No problem, Ma. I'll get one of the guys to bring your car to you later. Make sure it's locked." Ma dug her keys out of her huge ass purse and beeped the locks. We both got into the shop truck, and I started it up.

"Sure was nice of that Meg to help out. I don't know what I would have done without her."

"Yup, definitely nice of her." I shifted the truck into drive, keeping my foot on the brake, knowing exactly where mom was headed with this.

"You should ask her out." All I could do was shake my head and laugh.

"Straight to the point huh, Ma?"

"I'm old, I can say what I want. Meg is just the thing you need."

"I didn't know I needed anything." I pulled out of the parking lot and headed to Ma's house.

"You need someone in your life besides that club." My mom grabbed her phone out of her purse and started fiddling with it.

"We'll see, ma. Meg didn't seem too thrilled with me." She liked what she saw, but it was like she couldn't get away from me quick enough when she saw that Ma was going to be ok.

"Well, you are pretty intimidating, Lo. Thank goodness you didn't wear your cut."

My leather vest with my club rockers and patches was a part of me. "What the hell is wrong with my cut? If some bitch can't handle me in my cut, she sure as shit doesn't belong with me," I growled.

"Not what I meant Lo. That girl has been hurt, you can see it in her eyes. You'll have to be gentle with her."

My phone dinged. I dug it out of my pocket and saw my mom had texted me. "You texted me her number, ma?"

"Use it, Logan, fix her," she insisted.

I sighed and pulled into mom's driveway. "Maybe she doesn't want to be fixed, ma. Maybe she has a boyfriend."

"She doesn't. Call her, or I'll do it for you," she ordered.

I knew my mom's threat wasn't idle. She totally would call Meg and ask her out for me. Fuck. "I'll help you get your shit inside, ma."

"I'll make you lunch, and then you can call Meg," Ma said, as she jumped out of the truck and grabbed some bags.

I watched her walk into her house and looked at the message she had sent me. I saved Meg's number to my phone and grabbed the rest of Ma's shit and headed into the house.

Looked like I was calling Meg.

*

Meet Violet and Luke in the first chapter of DownShift!

**DownShift
Skid Row Kings
Book 1**

Winter Travers

Chapter 1

Violet

It was half past seven, and I should be on my way home already, but I wasn't.

I watched the lone girl who was sitting at the far table and sighed. She came in every day after school like clockwork, stayed till five forty-five then left. Except today, she didn't. The only way for me to get the heck out of here was to tell her the library was closing, but I didn't have the heart to.

She appeared to be well taken care of, nice clothes, good tennis shoes and well groomed. But she was never with anyone when she came in. Even when other kids would come in to work on homework or such, she stayed by herself at the far table.

I glanced at the watch on my wrist one last time and knew I had to go talk to her. All I wanted to do was go home, eat dinner, and take a nice long bath with my latest book boyfriend. Was that too much to ask?

After I skirted around the desk, I hesitantly made my way over to her, not wanting to tell someone they had to leave. I wasn't one for confrontation. "Um, excuse me."

The girl looked up at me and smiled. She couldn't have been more than thirteen, fourteen tops. Shiny braces encased her teeth, and black-rimmed glasses sat perched on her nose. "Yes?"

"The library closes at seven."

She glanced at the watch on her wrist and hit her hand on the table. "Crud. Luke was supposed to pick me up over an hour ago. I'm really sorry," she said, gathering her books and shoving them into her bag.

"Did you need to call him?"

"No, he probably won't answer the phone. He's only managed to pick me up once this week. He's busy getting ready for Street Wars. He's probably stuck under the hood of a car right now." She zipped her book bag shut and slung it over her shoulder. "I'm really sorry for keeping you here so late. I know the library closes at seven, but I was so into my book I didn't even notice the time."

"It's OK." I had totally been there before. That was the whole reason I worked at the library, I got to be surrounded by the things I loved all day.

"I'll see ya," she waved and headed out the door.

I quickly flipped off all the lights, making sure everything was ready for tomorrow and walked out the door. "Shit," I muttered as I got pelted with rain as I locked the door. I ran to my car, looking for the girl but didn't see her. Was she really going to walk home in the rain? I glanced up and down the street and saw her two blocks up, huddled under a tree.

Whoever this Luke was who was supposed to pick her up was a complete douche monkey for making this poor girl walk. I assumed it was her father, but it was strange that she called him Luke.

I ducked into my car, tossing my purse in the back and stuck the key in the ignition. I cranked it up and reversed out of my spot. As I pulled up to the girl, all I could do was shake my head. What did she think she was doing? Standing under a tree during a thunderstorm was not a bright idea.

"Get in the car," I hollered over the wind and rain. That was one of the drawbacks of the library, there weren't many windows so I never knew what the weather was like until I went outside. "I'll give you a ride."

She shook her head no and huddled under her jacket. What was she thinking? It didn't look like the rain was going to let up anytime soon. "I'm not supposed to ride with strangers."

Well, that was all fine and dandy except for the fact me being a stranger looked a lot better than standing in the rain. "You've been coming into the library for months. I'd hardly call us strangers."

"I don't even know your name," she said, her teeth chattering.

"It's Violet. Now get in the car."

She looked up and down the street, and it finally sunk in that I was her only chance of getting home not sopping wet. As she sprinted across the street, I reached across the center console and pushed open the passenger door.

"Oh my God, it's cold out there," she shivered as she slid in and closed the door.

"Well, it's only April. Plus, being soaking wet doesn't help."

She tossed her bag on the floor and rubbed her arms, trying to warm up. I switched the heat on full blast and pointed all the vents at her. She was dripping all over, and I knew the next person who sat there was going to get a wet ass. "Which way?"

"I live over on Thompson, on top of SRK Motors," she chattered.

I shifted the car into drive and headed down the street. "How come your dad didn't come and pick you up?" I asked, turning down Willow Street.

"Probably because he's dead."

Oh, crap. Whoopsie. "I'm sorry," I mumbled, feeling like an idiot. She seemed too young to have lost her dad.

"You can rule my mom out, too. They're both dead." She pulled a dry sweatshirt out of her bag and wrapped it around her hair, wringing it out.

OK. Well, things seemed to have taken a turn for the worse. "So, um, who's Luke? Your uncle?"

"No, he's my oldest brother. I've got three of them. They all work at the garage together that Luke owns, he's in charge."

"So, your brothers take care of you?"

"Ha, more like I take care of them. If it weren't for me, they'd spend all their time under the hood of a car."

"What's your name?" Here I was giving this girl a ride home, and I had no idea what her name was.

"Frankie."

"I'm Violet, by the way, if you didn't hear me before," I glanced at her, smiling.

"Neat name. Never heard it before." That would be because my mother was an old soul who thought to name me Violet would be retro. It wasn't. It was a color.

"Eh, it's OK."

I pulled up in front of the body shop and shut the car off. It was raining even harder now, the rain pelting against my windows. "I'll come in with you to make sure someone is home."

"I'm fourteen years old. I can be left alone.'

"Whatever. Let's go." She was right, but I didn't care. I was pretty pissed off that her brother had left her all alone to walk home in the rain.

We dashed to the door, my coat pulled over my head, and I stumbled into the door Frankie held open. "Oh my God, it's really coming down," I mumbled, shaking my coat off. My hair was matted to my forehead, and I'm sure I looked like a drowned rat.

"I think Luke is in the shop, I'll go get him." Frankie slipped through another door that I assumed lead to the shop, and I looked around.

Apparently, I was in the office of the body shop. There was a cluttered counter in front of me and stacks of wheels and tires all around. Four chairs are set off to the side, which I assume is the waiting area, and a vending machine on the far wall.

The phone rang a shrilling ring, making me jump. I looked around, trying to figure out what to do when the door to the shop was thrown open, and a bald, scowling man came walking through. He didn't even glance at me, just picked up the phone and started barking into it.

"Skid Row Kings," he grunted.

I couldn't hear what was being said on the other end, but I could tell Baldy was not happy. I looked down at my hands, noticing my cute plaid skirt I had put on that morning was now drenched and clinging to my legs. Thankfully I had worn flats today, or I probably would have fallen on my ass in the rain.

"What can I help you with?"

My head shot up, baldy staring at me. "Um, I brought Frankie home."

He looked me up and down, his eyes scanning me over. "Aren't you a little too old to be hanging out with a fourteen-year-old? You're what, sixteen, seventeen?"

"Try twenty-seven." This guy was a piece of work. He was looking me over like I was on display and he thought I was a teenager.

His eyes snapped to mine, and his jaw dropped. Yeah, jackass, I'm older than you are probably. "What the hell are you doing with Frankie?"

"She works at the library. You know, the place you promised to pick me up from today?" Frankie said, walking back into the shop. She had managed to find a towel and was drying herself off. I would kill for a towel right now.

"Fuck," Baldy twisted around and looked at the clock behind him. "Sorry, Frankie. Mitch and I were tearing apart the tranny on the Charger."

She waved her hand at him and tossed the towel to me. Oh, thank you sweet baby Jesus. I wiped the water that was dripping down my face and squeezed all the water out of my hair into it.

"How the hell did you get so wet if she gave you a ride home?"

"Because I started walking home, Luke, until Violet was kind enough to stop and give me a lift."

He watched me dry my hair, confusion on his face. "Violet?" he muttered.

"That's me," I said, sticking my hand out for him to shake. "I didn't want Frankie to get sick walking home. Plus, it's getting dark and someone her age shouldn't be out then."

"She's fourteen years old," he sneered. "I was out on the streets when I was twelve."

"Oh, well. If that's how you want to raise her." Luke was a gearhead that was also an ass. I didn't have time for this. My bath was definitely calling my name now that I was soaking wet. I tossed the towel back to Frankie and pulled my jacket over my head again. "You're welcome for bringing your sister home."

"I didn't ask you to."

"I know," I turned to Frankie and smiled. "I'll see ya tomorrow." She nodded her head at me, smiling, and I turned to walk out the door. I twisted the handle, and the door blew into me, rain pouring in. I glance back at Luke one time, a scowl on his face, and figured the pouring rain was better company than he was.

I pulled the door shut behind me and sprinted to my car, dodging puddles.

Once I was safely in my car, I looked up at the two-story building and sighed. I wish I could say this was a hole in the wall garage, but it was far from that. The building itself was a dark blue aluminum siding with huge neon letters that boasted, Skid Row Kings Garage, also known as SRK Garage. There were five bay doors that I'm assuming is where they pulled the cars into and over the office part is where I believe they lived. It was monstrous. Everyone in town took their cars here, especially the street racing crowd.

I had never been here before, mainly because I have never really needed repairs done on my car. I always went to the big chain stores to get my oil changed and thankfully hadn't needed any major repairs.

I started my car, thankful to be headed home. I turned around, the big looming building in my review as I headed down the street.

Hopefully, that was the last time I would ever step foot in Skid Row Kings garage and never see Luke again. He seemed like a total ass.

*

Check out The Karate Hotties!

Dropkick My Heart
Powerhouse MA
Book 1

Chapter 1

Kellan

"Left, Ryan." I shook my head and watched Ryan punch to the right. "Your other left, Ryan." In my fifteen years of teaching martial arts, I discovered left and right was a concept that was hard learned by anyone under the age of ten, especially when they were just excited to be punching and kicking the shit out of stuff.

"Okay! Lock it up." I stood in front of my class of twenty-five under belts and watched them all fall to the floor, eagerly looking up at me. I waited for all eyes to fall on me. "Good job today, guys. We need to work a bit longer on delta, but for only working on it one day, you guys are killing it." Clinton raised his hand eagerly, and I tipped my chin at him. "Go ahead, Clinton."

"Mr. Wright, when are we going to get to put all of the combos together?" he asked meekly.

"As soon as we learn them all," I assured him. Clinton asked the same question every class. The kid was the most eager to learn, but he had the attention span of a squirrel. I surveyed the class, then looked over the crowd of parents waiting to pick up their kids. "Now, remember that belt graduation is in three weeks, and you need to have your homework turned in before. Otherwise, you don't graduate." Everyone groaned at the word *homework*, and I couldn't help but smirk. They didn't have any clue how much homework I had done to reach sixth-degree black belt. "Everyone up," I said, motioning up with my hands. "And bow," I ordered, placing my hands at my sides and bowing.

All the kids started running up to me, giving me high fives and then scurrying off to their parents.

"Is Mr. Roman going to be here next time?" Carrie asked me as she high-fived me.

"He should be. He had a couple of things to do today and couldn't make it to class." Like sleeping until noon and screwing me over completely. Thankfully, it was the last class of the day, and I could hopefully find some time to sit down for five minutes.

Finally, the last parents left with their kids, and I locked the door behind them. I loved classes on Saturday, but they were exhausting when I was the only instructor.

The phone rang on the desk, and I knew it was Roman with some lame-ass excuse for why he didn't make it in today. Roman and I were business partners with Dante and Tate, but most of the time, it was all on me to make the school a success.

Roman's name flashed on the caller ID, and I picked up the phone. "So, what's your excuse this time?"

"Ugh, I'm fucking sick, man."

I shook my head and sat down behind the front counter. "That's called a hangover, Roman. Drink some fucking coffee, and get out of bed."

"Nah, man. This is worse than a hangover. I think I got food poisoning from the burger I ate last night at Tig's." Roman moaned into the phone, and I sighed.

Food poisoning from Tig's was a definite possibility. "I guess you should stop eating nasty shit while you're getting shit-faced every night."

"It's not every night," Roman grumbled.

"Sure, keep fucking telling yourself that."

Roman sighed. "Look, I was just calling to tell you sorry about not coming in today. If you wanna take off next Saturday, you can. I'll take care of the monsters all by myself."

"Nah, don't worry about." I made the mistake once of trying to take off a Saturday. Roman had called me halfway through the day, and I could barely hear him over yelling parents and screaming kids. I ended up coming in and spending most of the day putting out fires he had started between yelling at the kids and telling the parents to shut it while he was teaching. "Just get better, and I'll see you Monday night."

"What time do classes start?"

I closed my eyes and counted to ten. "Four. Same as every Monday," I reminded him.

"Got it. I'll be there."

I hung up the phone and sighed. Roman was one of the most talented guys I knew when it came to karate, but his adulting skills were severely lacking. At the age of twenty-eight, he should have his shit figured out.

When Roman, Tate, Dante, and I opened Powerhouse, we expected to help kids the way we were taught when we were young and just starting karate. Roman, Tate, and I began karate at the same time and worked our way through the belts together. Dante was a red belt when we were white belts, but he took us under his wing, and we all became close friends.

While Dante was almost ten years older than most of us, I was the highest black belt. Dante was a second-degree black belt, while Roman and Tate were fourth-degree. I was going for my sixth degree this year.

We all came together to start the school, because we all had our own specialties that, when put together, created a karate studio unlike any around. Dante was an international sparring champion six times over, while Roman and Tate were geniuses when it came to kamas and bo staff. I rounded us out with my expertise in forms and people skills the three others lacked at times.

The school had only been open for six months, but Dante and Tate already thought we needed to open another location. Not only had Roman bailed on me today, but so had Tate and Dante to go look at a space two towns over for a new studio.

I was in the minority when I said we should just focus on the Falls City school. Dante and Tate had decided between themselves that if we were doing so well here, another studio would be a goldmine. I didn't think they were wrong, I just wanted them to slow down, and wait for all of us to agree.

I threw my phone on top of a pile of new student paperwork and propped my arms on my head. I pushed off on the floor and spun around in the chair. Most days, it was hard to believe this was my life, and today was another one of those days. Dante, Tate, and Roman were my closest friends, but sometimes it felt like everything rested on my shoulders, while they were off somewhere enjoying life, and spending all the money we were making.

The days we didn't have classes, I was giving private lessons, or working on lesson plans for each class. Most of the time, the Kinder-kicker class was like herding a pack of cats that were all hyped up on catnip, and the Little Ninja class wasn't much better. Although, I still tried to teach them forms and basic karate to help them get to white belt. Once the kids hit white belt, things became more serious, and I buckled down on the curriculum.

The highest belt level we had right now was an orange belt, but in the stack of paper on the desk, there were three kids wanting to transfer over to Powerhouse. One of them was a purple belt, and the other two were red belts. I was rather shocked the two red belts wanted to transfer schools when they were close to being black belts, but I knew it was because in the short time we had been open, we already had a reputation of being the best.

If you were even a little bit into karate, you would have at least heard of one of us. We were the best, and we had the trophies and medals to prove it. That reputation was bringing in students left and right, but I couldn't keep doing this on my own anymore.

But, I wasn't going to stress about that right now, because a knock on the front door made me jump, and I turned to see my next private lesson through the glass.

My five-minute break was up, and it was back to the grind.

Someone had to make Powerhouse a success, and that someone was going to be me.

******

Get your engine running with the first book in
the
Nitro Crew Series!

Burndown
Nitro Crew Series
Book 1

Chapter 1

Remy

"You need to call your mother."

"I talked to her last week."

Lo cleared his throat. "We are talking about the same woman, right?"

"The woman who treats me like I'm thirteen and not twenty-six." I sighed and dropped the wrench on the workbench.

"Okay, we're talking about the same woman. So, you should know you need to call her, because if you don't call her, then I have to deal with her, and while I love the hell out of your mother, I don't want to deal with her like that."

"I'm well aware of the ways you like to handle my mother." I shook my head, still trying to remove the image of what I had walked in on the last time I had been home. Thank God I had only seen Lo's ass and my mom's hand waving frantically. "You guys really shouldn't do that on the kitchen table. People eat there."

"And most people knock before they walk into someone's house."

I ducked out the side door of the shop and leaned against the brick wall. "This is what you called to talk to me about?"

"When did you become such an asshole?"

"Got that from you," I mumbled.

"Humph. You might wanna tone that down when you're talking to me. I could kick your ass."

"I always do enjoy these talks, Lo." He was an ass half of the time, but he was a good guy. Plus, he kept my mom happy, so I couldn't really find any fault with him.

His deep chuckle traveled through the phone. "Just call your mom when you get the chance. And by that, I mean call her today."

He disconnected the call before I could say any more. That was his way. He said what he needed to, and that was it.

"Don't you think you should be working on the car instead of gabbing on the phone?"

I shoved my phone into my pocket and twisted around to see Roc walking across the parking lot with a cup of coffee in his hand. From talking to one asshole to another.

"Just talking to Lo."

"Should I care who Lo is?" He stood in front of me with his hand in his pocket, looking like the asshole he was—ripped and tattered jeans, black boots, and a tight shirt stretched across his chest. I don't think I have ever seen him in anything other than what he was wearing today other than the color of the shirt varying. Today, he had on the same blue as the main sponsor for the Brooks Cummings Racing Team. Also known as the race team I was finally part of.

I shook my head. "Probably not. Just my mom's husband."

"Well, you can chit-chat on your own time. Right now, I need that new engine dropped into the car before five. We have time at the track tomorrow afternoon to see if it'll run well enough for the first race of the season." Roc nodded to the shop. "Once the engine is dropped, you can help with the clutch."

Roc wandered off around the building, leaving me stewing.

This was my dream job, but I fucking hated it because it wasn't *exactly* how I'd imagined my dream job. I was working for a top five NHRA team, but all I did was assist the clutch and driveline specialist. That was the job I really wanted. A specialist.

I needed to be grateful for the job I had since I was one of the youngest pit crew guys out there, but damn if I didn't want more. I could do the job. I just needed to put in my time and prove that I was here to stay.

"Get to work, Grain," Roc called.

Son of a bitch. That guy was on me like white on rice. I looked around but didn't even see Roc. How the hell did he know I was still standing here if I couldn't even see him?

"You need me to talk to him? Ask him to go easy on you?"

Fucking Frankie. "Still think you showed him your tits to get on his good side."

She stuck her head out the side door and laughed. "He's too old for me. I'm more into guys who couldn't pass for being my dad."

"That picky attitude is what's keeping you from finding a guy, Frank."

She shook her head. "Probably has to do with the fact people call me Frank, and I always have grease under my nails."

I grabbed the rag out of my back pocket and tossed it at her. "That'll help."

She rolled her eyes. "A dirty shop towel sure is going to fix all of my problems." She held open the door. "You helping me get the computer hooked up would actually help me more."

"You really think they are going to let me help you? Roc thinks the only thing I'm good for is standing over Ronald and handing him a wrench now and then." I hadn't been as lucky as Frankie. We had both gone through High Performance Engine Building in school, along with ten other courses that had prepared us to be on the Cummings Racing Team, but Frankie had stood out with her natural ability with computers and her eye for detail.

"If Roc wants to get out of here before nine, he won't mind you helping me."

I rolled my eyes and slid past her into the shop. "You can argue with him over me helping you." My eyes fell on Ronald, who was bent over the engine. "I'm sure ol' Ronald is almost done, anyway. He even thinks it's dumb for me to watch him."

Frankie clapped me on the shoulder. "Ronald is old. Ronald will not be doing this job two years from now. When Ronald races off into the sunset, you and I both know this job is as good as yours."

"Two years, Frank? I don't wanna have to wait that long to do a job I can do right now."

We watched Ronald slowly stand up from the engine with his hand on his back. "I'm thinking you might just have to wait one season." She laughed and headed to the other side of the garage.

"Grain, you wanna come over here? I want you to make sure I got those nuts on tight enough," Roland called.

I sighed and hung my head. This is what I was getting paid for—tightening nuts. Not like I was making some grand salary, but I had hoped to be doing more than this.

Patience.

The only problem with being patient was, I wasn't.

*

93913335R00167

Made in the USA
Lexington, KY
19 July 2018